THE GHOST NETWORK

SYSTEM FAILURE

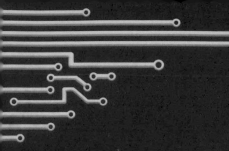

Other books in the series:
The Ghost Network: Activate
The Ghost Network: Reboot

Published by arrangement with Ferly.

The Ghost Network: System Failure copyright
© 2020 by I. I. Davidson. All rights reserved.
Printed in China. No part of this book may
be used or reproduced in any manner
whatsoever without written permission
except in the case of reprints in the context
of reviews.

Andrews McMeel Publishing
a division of Andrews McMeel Universal
1130 Walnut Street,
Kansas City, Missouri 64106

www.andrewsmcmeel.com

20 21 22 23 24 SDB 10 9 8 7 6 5 4 3 2 1
Paperback ISBN: 978-1-4494-9732-3
Hardback ISBN: 978-1-5248-5565-9
Library of Congress
Control Number: 2019954953

Made by:
King Yip (Dongguan) Printing & Packaging
Factory Ltd.
Address and location of manufacturer:
Daning Administrative District, Humen Town
Dongguan Guangdong, China 523930
1st Printing—1/13/20

Written by Gillian Philip
Series created by Ferly and Aleksi Delikouras

Editor: Jean Lucas
Designer: Tanja Kivistö
Art Director: Spencer Williams
Production Manager: Chuck Harper
Production Editor: Amy Strassner

ATTENTION: SCHOOLS AND BUSINESSES
Andrews McMeel books are available at
quantity discounts with bulk purchase
for educational, business, or sales
promotional use. For information,
please e-mail the Andrews McMeel Publishing
Special Sales Department:
specialsales@amuniversal.com.

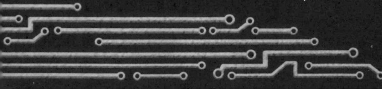

THE GHOST NETWORK

SYSTEM FAILURE

I. I. DAVIDSON

Andrews McMeel
PUBLISHING®

65°45'12.9"N
168°55'55.2"W

THE MA'YAARR COMPLEX

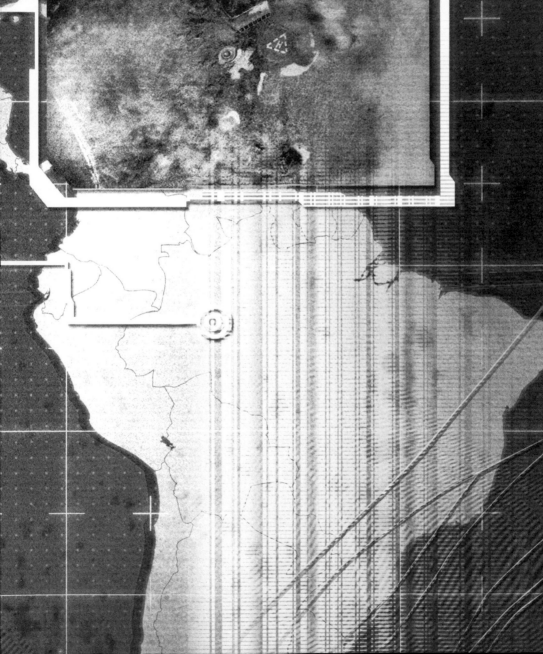

WOLF'S DEN

Prologue

"I hope we didn't make a mistake leaving the tour group." Francisco frowned at his cell phone. "We'll have to be careful, Juliana. Stray from the right coordinates and we might never find our way out of this forest. Afonso was pretty clear about that."

Juliana shoved aside the thick stalks of a heliconia and caught up with her husband. "If Afonso was even his real name," she muttered. "I'm not even sure he was Brazilian. But we didn't have a choice, Francisco. We need to find her."

"I know." Her husband laid his arm around her shoulders. He meant it to be comforting, she knew, but it only made her feel hotter and stickier than ever.

"If we don't," she told him, pulling gently away, "I don't care if we get lost. She's all that matters, Francisco." Juliana wiped the sweat from her eyes. "If this Afonso was telling the truth, you just have to input the coordinates without any mistakes."

"I'm being careful—believe me." He gave her a lopsided grin and then walked ahead. "And the coordinates are exactly as he wrote them down. But I don't see anything . . ."

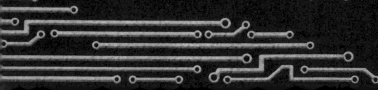

Juliana hurried after him, brushing spiderwebs out of her way. The truth was that she had to strain to hear what her husband was saying. The level of noise in the rain forest was unbelievable. She had expected wildlife—but not quite so much of it. The racket of what seemed like a million insects was right in her ear; the constant chirping of cicadas, the piping of tree frogs, and the *tonk-tonk-tonk* of bellbirds resounded and echoed from the dense foliage. In the distance, howler monkeys boomed and hooted.

"It's worse than Rio at rush hour," she called lightly.

"What did you say?" Francisco half turned toward her, then snapped his head back ahead in a double take. She saw him punch the air in triumph; his fist caught a broad bromeliad leaf that showered water over him, but he seemed not to notice.

"Juliana! There's something here!"

"*Graças a deus*," she murmured. They'd been trekking through this terrifying jungle since before dawn, and the sun had long ago sunk from the patch of sky barely visible through the thick canopy. She'd been afraid they would find nothing before nightfall, which was supposed to be for cocktails and delicate *petiscos*, little snacks, on the balcony by their pool at the São Paulo villa. The thought of a long night alone in the vicinity of where anacondas, jaguars, and pit vipers lived made her shudder.

Juliana pulled up the straps on her backpack and clambered over a fallen log to Francisco's side. His eyes shone as he pushed aside a soursop branch to reveal strands of shining barbed wire. She gasped.

"That's a new fence," he said in a low voice. "This has to be the right place, and it's exactly where Afonso told us it would be."

<7>

Juliana lifted her head to stare up at the top of the fence. It might be new, but it was already entangled with vines and spiderwebs of the forest. Passionflowers drooped from the top-most strands; it made her nervous, as if the fence were making a strong effort to hide its forbidding purpose. "How will we get over that?"

"Follow it around?" he suggested. "We're bound to find a gate somewhere. Are you ready for this?"

Juliana straightened her shoulders. Her backpack straps dug into her flesh, and her green shirt was drenched with sweat, but none of that mattered. "We have to be," she said firmly. "I won't leave here without her. We've searched too long to give up now."

Francisco nodded. Pulling a machete from his belt, he began to hack at the foliage, which seemed even thicker along the fence. Juliana, desperate not to lose sight of the fence, touched every steel post as they reached it, not caring when she scratched her hand on barbs and drew blood. *We're so close now. I can feel it.* Her heart throbbed with fear and excitement at the same time.

Panting, Francisco paused and gestured past the fence. "It's clearer here," he gasped. "Look."

Leaning close to the wire, Juliana peered through.

Her heartbeat lightened and quickened. If this was where their daughter had been living, it wasn't so bad. It was quite charming, in fact. The palm-thatched wicker huts looked straight out of a gap year tourist brochure. A glittering waterfall tumbled from a rockface into a turquoise pool surrounded by flowering bromeliads and orchids; green streams traversed through verdant bushes to and from the lake. Above the pool she caught sight of wooden walkways, suspended on thick ropes between

<8>

the huts; butterflies flitted between the walkways and the flowers below. A hummingbird darted over to a passionflower and hovered there, feeding. Juliana was sure she could smell the blossom, despite the thick scent of moist soil and decaying plants that permeated the rain forest.

"It's beautiful," she whispered to Francisco.

"Yes. But still no gate." He frowned again at his cell phone screen. "This *has* to be the place. If this was a tourist resort, it would be full of . . . well, tourists." He shrugged in bewilderment.

"I'm sure she's here. I'm sure of it! Francisco, we *must* find a way—"

"What are you doing here?"

The words were soft, spoken in the high voice of a child, but were filled with a distinct menacing tone. Juliana spun around in shock, almost tripping over a root. She stared in shock at the boy who emerged from the trees behind them.

She vaguely noticed his shock of black hair bound back by a tie-dyed bandana and his dark eyes blazing beneath. He was wearing a loose and ragged vest top and jungle-patterned board shorts that were a little too big.

But Juliana's true focus was on the gun the boy held in both his small hands. It was pointing right at her, and the barrel did not tremble in the slightest.

"I said, 'What are you doing here?'" the boy repeated, his eyes narrowing. *He couldn't be more than twelve years old*, she thought in disbelief. "And who are you?"

"We, uh—" Francisco pushed forward a little to stand in front of his wife for protection. She could feel him trembling, even

<9>

though she herself was shaking too. "We don't mean any harm! We're—we're looking for our daughter."

The boy stared at them both in silence. His finger rubbed the gun's trigger thoughtfully, and Juliana thought her pounding heart might explode.

"Here, I'll show you, I—" Francisco reached into his shirt pocket.

The boy tensed. He raised the gun slightly and steadied its aim right between Francisco's eyes. Juliana gave a stifled cry.

"No!" gasped Francisco. "A photo, a picture." He tapped his cell phone with shaking fingers and held it out to the boy, screen-first. "Our daughter, see? We're looking for her. That's all!"

"We've lost her, for so very long," blurted Juliana. "Please . . . we don't want any trouble. We just want to find her!"

The boy still said nothing. He stared hard at the image, his brow creasing.

If she is here, thought Juliana, *this boy must know her.* Her daughter was unmistakable—her shining hair, those fierce eyes, the surly but beautiful mouth. *Unless she's changed so much that we wouldn't recognize her anymore. . . .* Something twisted painfully inside Juliana's chest as she considered this truth.

"This is your daughter?" snapped the boy suddenly. He raised his eyes to glare at Juliana. "You're sure?"

Of course I'm sure! But Juliana tightened her lips and simply nodded.

An even more suspicious look filled the boy's eyes now, if that were even possible. He jerked the gun, and Juliana heard Francisco gasp.

<10>

"You come with me," commanded the boy, gesturing with the gun along the fence. "Walk ahead. I'll tell you where to go."

Juliana's back twitched as she walked ahead of the boy. If his finger slipped on that trigger—of a gun that looked too heavy for him—it would all be over. She felt Francisco's fingers entwine hers and hold them tightly, as they stumbled through the undergrowth along the fence.

When the gate finally came into sight, it was huge and intimidating, barred and locked. However, as the boy urged them forward, it slowly swung open. If she didn't believe that she might find her daughter here, Juliana would never have found the courage to walk through it.

Some unknown threat suddenly made her spine tingle, and, for a fleeting moment, even took her mind off the gun behind her. She glanced to the side, toward a slow green river that coiled through the camp like a vast snake. Her throat went dry, and she blinked as she tried to peer harder.

Were those lights she could see in the water? A piercing shiver filled her. No. Not lights, surely, not arranged as they were in such close pairs.

And now Juliana was sure of it: they were not lights but eyes that glowed with a piercing hostility. Red eyes, blinking slowly, and lurking just beneath the murky surface.

<11>

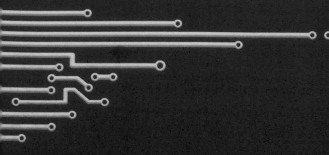

One

Eva Vygotsky stared out across the choppy waters of the Bering Strait toward Big Diomede, as the brisk wind blustered her hair and stung her eyes. Even in the late summer, there was a chill in the air, but she didn't mind. She needed to be far from those adolescent fools in the Center—students *and* teachers—far from air-conditioning, central heating, and electric lighting. The breeze helped clear her head; she needed the sharp sting on her skin to help her think astutely about that email.

She couldn't stop herself from looking at it again. Opening up her phone, she clicked the Mail icon and opened it.

Yes, an old-fashioned email and from an old-school establishment: the FBI.

Dear Ms. Vygotsky,

We have tried to contact you for some time, without success, to inform you that we have reason to believe your parents are currently searching for you.

Owing to the ambiguity surrounding your whereabouts, and the time sensitivity of this situation, we have instructed your parents to

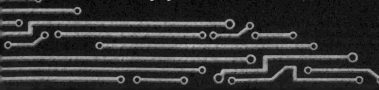

meet you at a location owned by your legal guardian, Mikael Laine. This location, the Ma'yaarr Complex in Amazonas, Brazil, has been agreed upon by Mr. Laine. You will receive all further instructions from him.

Please make your way to the agreed location at your earliest opportunity. You will be permitted to bring a small group of trusted friends with you; indeed, owing to the nature of the journey, this is strongly recommended.

Should you require any assistance, please make contact with the person named at the bottom of this letter.

Eva let her eyes drift back to the top of the email, and she read it again. Then once more. Her sheer disbelief was making it hard for the words to sink in. It was surprising enough that anyone outside the walls of the Wolf's Den was aware of her existence. But someone had made contact with her *parents?* It was too much to fathom that her parents had done the contacting.

She hadn't seen them in—oh, how long? She'd almost let herself forget their existence. After all, she'd managed to persuade herself that they had forgotten all about her. Why else would they have left her alone in the world for so long? Why would they have abandoned her, alone in a train car on the Trans-Siberian Express, to be found by the first bureaucratic agent of the state who happened along? And then passed along to some tech genius in search of experimental guinea pigs?

Eva gritted her teeth and swallowed the bitterness. It hadn't been so bad, had it? Mikael and his fellow scientists might have done something very strange to her brain, but at least she'd finally been *wanted.*

<13>

No, she told herself. *Stop that.* If it hadn't been for Mikael Laine and his experimental biology, and his Ghost Network gang of DNA-altered superteens, she wouldn't have met her best friends in the world. Her *only* friends in the world, to be honest.

Eva shook herself. It was so hard to fight back the negative thoughts, but she had something more important to think about now: this plan, created (as usual) without her knowledge, and (as usual) coordinated by Mikael. Rolling her eyes, she pulled her sweater around her tighter and peered at the email again.

At least it was a plan, a development. School life at the Wolf's Den had grown almost monotonous in the past six months: study, revision, exams; rinse and repeat till the year-end finals. After their adventures in Morocco, when she and Mikael had had to race from Alaska to meet the Ghost Network as they escaped the clutches of Roy Lykos's goons at the Scarab's Temple, the past half year had seemed almost . . . boring.

Maybe it hadn't been boring for the others. Akane and Slack had been delighted to spend the summer break with their families in Alaska and Tokyo. Salome had been downhearted and pensive on her return from Ethiopia, but only because she was already missing her parents and siblings. And John Laine hadn't wanted to come home from his vacation at all—he'd had six weeks of normal life in Anchorage with his mother and sister—and hadn't stopped complaining since. *I got to be normal all summer. I got to play Xbox games and shoot people and fight battles, and it was all FICTION. And I had to come back here where I'm nothing but a walking, talking prototype weapon that my dad invented!*

<14>

Eva smirked to herself. It was a bit bold of John to think he had the monopoly on resentment. After all, Mikael Laine's process hadn't even turned Eva into an *efficient* superbeing. She was no more than a flawed prototype for the others. But if anybody was more bitter than Eva about becoming a DNA-enhanced superbeing, it was Mikael's actual son. Maybe that was because John remembered his "real life." Eva had never had a "normal life" to miss.

That thought brought her sharply back to the email. She scowled at it, scrolling it up and down with her thumb. John's father might have conducted dangerous experimental DNA processes on him and his friends—but only to save their lives after lethal accidents. John, Slack, Salome, and Akane at least still had loving families who cared about them—*they* hadn't been dumped in some strange train car.

So why had her parents completely vanished? Where had they been for all these years? Had Eva even crossed their minds at any time? Why would they suddenly reappear?

I don't belong in the Ghost Network, not really. Mikael's work on me was only experimental. I'm nothing but an inconvenience. . . . A chill shivered down Eva's spine that had nothing to do with the sea breeze. *But I don't really belong with my parents either, do I?*

But maybe now I can find them and ask them. Her jaw clenched.

Suddenly feeling rather decisive, Eva stuffed her phone in her pocket and hurried back to the stairwell that led to the underground complex of the Wolf's Den. Anyway, it was time for the opening assembly for the year. The other students already thought she was quite strange; she didn't want them to notice her missing *this important event.*

<15>

Halfway down the clear Perspex ramp that circled the atrium, Eva spotted Salome ahead of her. Her elegant braided head, held almost arrogantly high, was unmistakable.

"Salome, wait!"

The girl turned, and her happy smile shattered any illusion of standoffish arrogance. "Eva! Where have you been?"

"Outside. Thinking." Hesitantly, Eva returned Salome's hug. "In fact, you are the very person I wanted to see. I need to ask your opinion."

"You know I'm always happy to give that." Salome winked solemnly.

"Good, because you're usually wise." Eva opened the email and handed her phone to Salome. "Look at this and tell me what you think."

"Wow. I didn't even know there was a Center in the Amazon. That's exciting in itself." Salome then fell silent for long pauses, staring intently at the screen as they walked side by side. At last she glanced up at Eva, her eyes bright.

"This is wonderful news, Eva. Your parents are looking for you. Between the FBI and Mikael, they're bound to bring you together!" Salome stopped and flung her arms around Eva. "I'm so happy for you!"

"I'm not so sure," growled Eva quietly. "How do I know these people are for real? I myself wouldn't know whether these supposed parents of mine are impostors. Would the FBI? Would Mikael?"

"I don't think either of them would treat this lightly." Salome clasped Eva's hands. "You can be fairly sure they'll have checked their identities, Eva. Look at it this way." She smiled. "No one else

<16>

even knows you exist, so why would someone plan a complex hoax to find you? It *has* to be your mother and father."

"You really think so?" asked Eva doubtfully. "I'm scared to believe it. What about Roy Lykos?" The former departmental head at the Wolf's Den had, after all, been the puppet master of everyone who had threatened Eva and her friends so far. "Couldn't he have masterminded this, like he did in Morocco? And here at school? Lykos has never stopped wanting to control the Ghost Network."

Salome shook her head firmly. "He's been safely locked up in San Quentin since Morocco," she assured Eva. "He might get away with a lot of things and have incredible government contacts, but even he can't get away with murder. And it was you that put him in jail, Eva, when you filmed him shooting the helicopter pilot. Be proud—and believe in your parents! I think it's worth the risk, don't you?"

Gazing into Salome's shining eyes, Eva felt her hopes rising. Slowly, she nodded. "Yes. Yes, all right, Salome. I'll dare to believe it—for now." She managed a smile.

"And we can all rest easy for a while," added Salome. "Lykos can't scheme with any more of his minions from a cell in San Quentin—and he can hardly come after us himself. For once we can concentrate on our studies in peace, yes?"

"Well . . ." Eva took her phone back and studied the email. "I do have this, and that might get in the way of Ms. Reiffelt's hacking classes for a while . . ."

"Oh, yes!" Salome released Eva and clapped her hands in delight. "Mikael's going to want us to start planning a little field trip to Brazil. And even *I* won't miss Howard McAuliffe's coding lectures!"

<17>

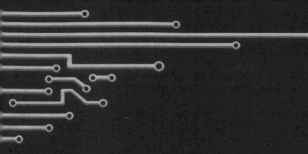

Two

It was Mikael's first welcome address for a full term— he had taken over as principal after the events in the Sahara midway through the summer term—and the student body seemed determined to give him a resounding official endorsement. As he strode onto the platform, his ashy-blond hair swept back neatly and his gray-blue eyes gleaming with amusement, the noise from the packed atrium was deafening: screams of approval, roars of delight, stamping, clapping, and whooping.

He might as well be their god, thought John Laine bitterly. *Their tin-pot little techie idol. They couldn't be any more obsequious.*

"I feel sorry for Irma Reiffelt," he muttered to Slack. "She had all the experience, and she knew this school inside out. Why should she have to step aside to make way for my dad?"

"Ms. Reiffelt did the honorable thing," Salome reminded him softly. "Roy Lykos was operating right under her nose, running all his schemes from this school."

"And she made way for Mikael voluntarily," added Slack. "It's not like she was fired."

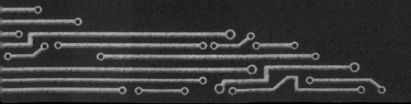

"It's still wrong," growled John. "Dad and Roy started all this, my dad with his stupid experiments and Lykos with his evil plans. I still don't think Irma Reiffelt should have to pay for their mistakes."

"His stupid experiments saved all our lives," Akane reminded him. "We'd all be dead if he hadn't invented the AI transfusion and figured out how to combine it with our DNA."

"Sure, he wasn't acting selfishly *at all*," said John sarcastically. He glared up at his father, who was now flapping his arms ineffectually and laughing as he tried to calm the cheering students.

"I think it's kind of funny how they all adore your dad," insisted Slack. "And it's one in the eye for Roy Lykos. Talk about a fallen hero."

"Well, exactly," said John, still sulking. "They worshipped Lykos too—remember? And look what *he* did."

"Oh, don't take it so seriously, John." Slack nudged him hard with his elbow. "It's kind of nice for your dad to get some recognition. We don't have to join in, and neither do you."

John sat back and folded his arms, scowling. The students were quiet now and eager to hear what Mikael had to say, and then Mikael himself started talking. He covered all the usual inspirational start-of-term stuff about effort and excellence. John shut out the familiar voice, determined not to listen to a word.

He still resented the way his mother had welcomed Mikael back with open arms and barely a question asked. Tina had been so overjoyed to know her husband was alive after all that she had barely quizzed him about what he'd been up to. *I know your father better than anyone, John,* she'd told him sternly. *And if he says*

<19>

he was forced to disappear, I believe him. He must have had good reasons. He loves us, and I know he did what was best for all of us.

Ugh. John shuddered with disgust at the memory. He'd always thought his mom was a *feminist.*

"And I'm especially keen for the girls here to show me what you can do," Mikael was emphasizing. "Don't let yourselves be talked over in class—I know the boys can be a bit full of themselves"—hearty student laughter—"but some of our most promising students this year are female. Computers may have been largely a man's world until recently, but we at the Wolf's Den aim to change that!"

John let the roar of the applause wash over him and kept his arms tightly folded. He tuned out his father's voice again.

Slack's made me watch enough stupid rom-coms, he thought. *Isn't it always the smart woman who figures out the bad guy? It's the starry-eyed son who never sees anything wrong with his father! But not when it comes to my mother, oh no . . .*

"It's not as if he's changed," he growled to Slack. "He's the same workaholic he always was. No time for his family even though he *made himself* dead to us for years. All he thinks about is the Centers and getting them back to what *he* wanted them to be. An elite group of tech schools or, in other words, a vehicle for his ambitions instead of Lykos's! I might as well still be lost in the Sahara for all he cares. I don't think he even knows I'm mad at him."

Slack gave him a piercing, sidelong gaze. "Maybe he doesn't want to notice," he murmured. "You've been pretty surly around him. It's not like you encourage any father-son interaction."

"Not my job," grunted John.

<20>

Slack gave an emphatic sigh and turned back to Mikael, who was well into his stride now.

"I have several exciting new projects to announce," grinned Mikael, brandishing a thin sheaf of paper. "These were the ideas that came out of our summer project competition—thank you to all who entered, and congratulations to the winning suggestions. Adam Kruz and Leo Pallikaris, please stand up!"

John couldn't help but let out a short gasp. His stomach felt cold. Adam and Leo? Roy Lykos's pet mini-henchmen? *And Dad knows that! What's he thinking?* As the two boys rose to their feet, they looked even more smug and supercilious than usual, and that was saying something.

"Adam and Leo—you and your team came up with a terrific concept, and we want to take it forward." Mikael smiled and spread his hands to encompass the entire hall. "This team wants to bring AI to animals. Not real ones—before you all get PETA on the phone—but robotic animals that exactly resemble their natural counterparts." Nodding happily, he waited for the cries of excitement to die down. "Now, I know that some of the younger classes had suggested a school team of huskies for the winter months. Not very practical, I'm afraid—not for real dogs. But over the summer, this project group has created a prototype pack of robo-huskies that are a whole lot more appropriate to Little Diomede." Mikael took a deep breath and swept his hand toward the ramps that circled the atrium.

"Ladies, gentlemen—I present: the K9 Krew!"

Overcome with curiosity, John couldn't help but stare as the robots appeared, vague and blurred by the Perspex below them.

<21>

As the six "dogs" stalked downward and became fully visible, he sucked in an astonished breath.

The whole atrium was gaping in fascination. John had expected at least the click of metal feet, but the robots' paws padded along in silence. They certainly were prototypes—nobody would want to pet those black steel limbs or the doglike metal heads—but they moved exactly like huskies, legs smooth and natural. The leader turned its head toward the students; sharp ears pricked and swiveled, and its eyes glowed red. To John there was a sinister sense of actual, sentient life in its emotionless stare.

"How in the world did Adam and Leo . . ." breathed Slack, but his voice dried. He shook his head. "Those are the *coolest things ever.*"

"We'll be improving the prototype as part of the project," explained Mikael. "Who knows—we might even manage a fur pelt by the end of term, and then our dogs might seem friendlier!" The students laughed. "So if anyone here has ever had a yearning to work with animals, sign up on the online forms for Project Husky!"

"That'll be me!" yelped Slack, leaping from his seat with his arm raised.

Mikael grinned. "Like I said, register on the intranet site after this assembly, Slack. But I know for a fact you'd enjoy this one. Why don't you join Leo and Adam and their team right now? We're going to have our first 'husky safari' on the plateau, and any interested students are welcome to participate."

John stared in disbelief as, without a backward glance, Slack rushed off toward the gathering group of excited students at the edge of the atrium. *Gee. Thanks, pal.*

<22>

Arms were shooting up all over the crowd. Mikael nodded indulgently at a younger student.

"Would this process be applicable to other kinds of animals?" The girl's eyes shone.

"Sure! Why not? If someone builds the animal robots, we can develop the appropriate AI." Mikael grinned. "Bring on the robot hamsters!"

There were squeals of excited laughter from the tenth graders. But Mikael grew solemn again, shuffling his papers.

"Hamsters, and who knows what after that. . . . I'm sure you all have many questions and comments, and I'd expect nothing less from Wolf's Den students." Mikael's eyes caught John's, and he smiled. "Right now, though, I want to move on to the second prizewinning project. I hope you won't think I'm indulging in any nepotism when I say this team was led by John Laine!"

Uproarious applause ensued. John rolled his eyes. Of course they wouldn't think Mikael was biased. Apparently, he could do no wrong in their eyes.

"John, why don't you join me on the platform to help me explain the MindReader?"

John froze for a moment. He didn't like the spotlight anyway. But at that moment, fierce resentment was warring inside him with delight that his project had been chosen. Gripping the sides of his chair, he made himself stay in place.

"It's an excellent project," enthused Mikael, staring slightly perplexed at his son. "And I'm not just saying that as a proud dad, because every member of the team contributed. The MindReader team has proposed a groundbreaking form of communication: 'voluntary telepathy.'" He held out his hand, palm upward, and

<23>

heads craned to see. "You won't be able to make it out, but this is a chip that can be placed behind the ear." Mikael gestured at the screen behind him. "You can see the original basic blueprint here. The chip picks up vibrations in the brain to imitate a conversation without the need for either an external device or a spoken voice. The device works worldwide and is being issued this term by students at all the Centers."

"Oohs" and "aahs" erupted from the wide-eyed student body. Mikael nodded modestly. John gritted his teeth. *Yeah, look modest. It may be based on the tech you used on me, but it was me who did all the work over the summer.*

"John!" His father's enthusiastic voice interrupted his resentful thoughts. "John, come on up here and take a bow!"

John locked eyes with his father. There was something pleading in Mikael's expression. John got to his feet.

"John?" Mikael looked relieved. "That's it, come and get some appreciation for all your hard work!"

Slowly, John shook his head. Turning on his heel, he shoved his way past Salome and Akane. Then he pushed through the silent, astonished students and stormed out of the atrium.

<24>

Three

The corridor was deserted; that wasn't surprising, thought John sourly, since everybody was in the atrium worshipping at the feet of Mikael Laine. That was fine by him; he didn't want to see anyone. The students in this Center were supposed to be so smart, yet all of them—Slack too!—went soft in the head for a charismatic leader. *No wonder Roy Lykos got such a firm hold of everybody. They'll all believe anything.*

No, that wasn't fair. His dad could be a selfish jerk, but he was no Roy Lykos. John took a deep breath and tried to repress his churning anger. He glanced to the side as he passed the broad entrance to the staff corridor.

There was someone standing outside Mikael's office. Although those supercomfortable, bubble-shaped white pods were available, she hadn't chosen to sit in one; she was propped idly against the opaque glass wall, the fringe of her black bobbed hair falling over her eyes as she peered at her tablet.

"Sarah? I mean, Ms. Lopez?" John perked up. Despite his mood, he didn't want to look sulky in front of the young reporter, who had gotten her first big break through the Ghost Network and was

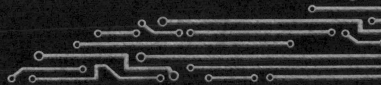

now a rising star in online journalism. Apart from wanting to look professional, he was well aware he had a hopeless crush on her. Sarah Lopez glanced toward him, her frown clearing.

"You know *Sarah* is fine, John," she grinned. Lazily she blew the fringe out of her black-rimmed eyes. "How's it going with you?"

"Great," lied John. "Exciting start of a new term and all that. What are you doing here?"

"Waiting to interview your dad." She shrugged and grinned again. "Been waiting awhile. He's a busy man, your father."

John gritted his teeth in a bland smile. "He sure is. What's the interview for?"

"Man of the Year in the *Alaska Star*," she told him. "Next up: *Time* magazine, if he keeps going on this trajectory. His connection with Roy Lykos—the AI research, going into hiding, but *especially* nearly being murdered by Roy—is turning a regular business story into a sensation."

John couldn't control himself any longer. "Man of the Year," he almost spat. "For machines maybe. His family, less so."

He didn't pause to absorb the astonishment on Sarah's face. Turning around quickly, he strode as rapidly as he could toward the stairwell.

Sarah didn't call after him, and he didn't blame her. He must look like your standard surly teenager, John thought, and he could even imagine her rolling her eyes. But right now, he didn't care. Taking the stairs two at a time, he swept the chip embedded in his palm across the reader and pushed through into the blustery open air.

The bright freshness was always a little startling after the climate-controlled school, and John sucked in a huge lungful

<26>

of it. Quite suddenly, he was certain: he'd had enough. He'd had enough of the Wolf's Den and its suffocating elitism. Anger hot in his throat, he strode across the plateau, hands in his pockets; he was barely able to catch a glimpse of the expansive ocean.

Nobody else ever seemed to come here. Well, maybe Eva sometimes; like him, she seemed to enjoy reminding herself that there was life beyond the Wolf's Den. *And there's life outside the Ghost Network too*, he reminded himself angrily. Sure, he and his friends might have done some good as part of Mikael's team of AI-enhanced superteens. But he couldn't help constantly feeling as if he were being used. *By his own dad!*

The fact that he saved his life should be taken into account with the other data—

"Oh, shut up, IIDA!" he barked aloud. He was in no mood to listen to the Ghosts' supercomputer "mother" inside the Center.

Even if it might just be his own conscience talking . . .

"I said shut up!" Deliberately, he clicked off the voice in his head.

It had been so good to spend time at home over the summer, being a normal son and brother in a normal family, with all its squabbles and all the "boring" day-to-day life. After a few days of that, he'd realized just how much he missed it. If he let himself mope too much, he would begin to see that he didn't want to be here at the Wolf's Den anymore . . .

"John? Where are you going?"

He started. He hadn't even heard Akane's approach. She stared at him in bemusement, her choppy red hair tangled by the wind.

"Were you heading for the harbor?"

He glanced down at the steep slope in front of him. Far below, the little port of Diomede City nestled in its bay. "I guess I was. I've had enough of this place, Akane."

<27>

"Had enough of what?" She snorted. "The finest education a hacker could ask for? A luxury educational Center with the best teachers in the world? Don't be so dumb!"

"I hate it here! And I think I hate my dad even more."

"No, you don't." Akane's face set hard, and she folded her arms. "You're just feeling sorry for yourself, and you're mad at your dad. You'll get over it. I know you, John."

"You hardly know me at all! We met like a year ago!" Even as he said it, John felt a twist of guilt. It wasn't really true.

"And a long time before that online. You were telling me all your inner thoughts and feelings before you were ten! So don't pull that line with *me*, John Laine!"

They glared at each other for a long, angry moment.

"Then you know I can't take any more of this," he blurted at last. "I've had it with Dad, with the Wolf's Den, the Ghost Network—everything! I'm gonna find a boat."

He shoved past her, but she was far too agile to lose her balance. She simply twisted with him, and before he knew what was happening, her slender arm was around his neck, wrenching him down into a headlock. He wriggled in indignation, but her grip was firm.

"I hate you, Akane!" he gurgled furiously.

"Nah, you don't." Letting him go, she slapped him affectionately on the shoulder. "And you know as well as I do you're not going anywhere."

"Don't know your own strength," he growled, rubbing his throat as he got shakily to his feet.

"I didn't hurt you one bit," she said airily. "Except your pride, of course, but that's always been kinda sensitive. Come on, I'll walk you back to the Center."

<28>

Grudgingly, he fell in behind her. The annoying thing was he knew she was right. She *did* know him better than anyone, and it *would* be stupid and cowardly to run away.

In the distance, but growing swiftly nearer, John heard the rattle of rotors. He paused, panting, and turned to peer into the cloud-spattered sky.

A black dot was approaching the island, growing swiftly to become a recognizable helicopter. It was one of the ones that flew out of Wales Airport; John recognized the serial number. The Wolf's Den used the company for ferrying students at the beginning and end of term; John could almost smell the familiar hot steel and aluminum and the plastic of the uncomfortable seat pads.

The aircraft roared above them, whipping their hair in the downdraft. It was heading for the Wolf's Den helipad on the plateau, and John felt a cold clenching sensation in his gut.

It wasn't Roy Lykos; it couldn't be. He was locked safely in a state penitentiary. There was no danger of him returning to the island to seize the Ghost Network and turn them for his own purposes.

But the instinctive, atavistic fear reminded John of what a danger the man had once been. *I don't trust that he's gone forever. I can't.*

So he had to admit it: Akane was right. Despite the oppressive demands of his own father, he was better off to stick with his friends in the Ghost Network.

Strength in numbers, John reminded himself with a foreboding shiver. *Strength—and safety too.*

<29>

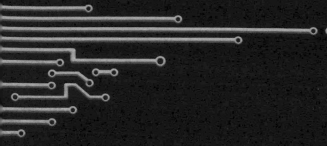

Four

Students were rising from the assembly, gathering books and jackets and laptops, gossiping excitedly as they made their way in a slow-moving crowd toward lecture halls, theaters, and dorm rooms. Salome stretched her aching shoulders and smiled at Eva.

"That was quite the performance from Mikael. They all seemed to like it, though."

"Yeah." Eva shrugged. "It was pretty good. But I think we know him too well to be quite *that* starstruck." She gestured with a thumb at the small cluster of younger students who were gathered around Mikael, asking questions and gazing up at him with shining eyes.

"Hmph." Salome gave a short laugh as the two girls walked out of the atrium side by side. "I do think John's too hard on him, though. When did John turn into such a surly emo?"

Eva rolled her eyes. "He is a teenage boy, Salome. What did you expect?"

"Well, I'm looking forward to the term," Salome said cheerfully, hugging her laptop against her. "We can do so much with the MindReader tech, Eva! It's got so many possibilities—"

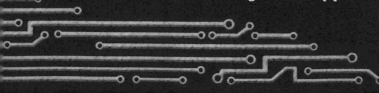

Ahead of them, Mikael's office door crashed open. Mikael must have overridden the electronic mechanism, because the sleek wood slammed and shuddered as it hit the outer wall. Salome's mouth fell open.

"What the—"

"*Get out!*" barked a familiar voice, one that was usually gentle and amused. Not right now, it wasn't. "Get out of this Center, Sarah Lopez. And don't let me see your face on my property again!"

Sarah Lopez was backing out of the office, her tablet clutched against her chest, but she was glaring at its occupant, unintimidated. "I'll go. But you can't muzzle the press. Not all of us and not forever. One day the world's going to see Mikael Laine for what he really is!"

Salome and Eva exchanged horrified glances.

"Salif!" Mikael barged out of his office, almost sweeping Sarah aside.

The tall Moroccan security guard came around the far corner at a hasty jog. "Mr. Laine? What's up?"

"This so-called journalist. Get her off this island now, Salif. Escort her to the helipad. I don't want her feet to touch the ground till she lands in Wales."

"You got it, Mikael." With a nod, Salif took Sarah's elbow. She shook him off and marched furiously ahead of him toward the helipad stairwell.

"Sarah! What's going on?" Salome hurried to follow her, forced to jog to keep up with Salif's long stride. He glanced down at her, mildly irritated.

"Nothing," snapped Sarah, glaring straight ahead. "Nothing I can say right now, anyway. Don't worry, Salome; I'm happy

<31>

to leave." For a moment she halted and spun to face Salome. "Or maybe you *should* worry a little. You should know Saint Mikael Laine isn't exactly what—or who—he's cracked up to be."

"What?" blurted Salome again. But Salif had already urged Sarah Lopez on.

"Come on, young lady," he muttered. "Don't make this hard on both of us."

Salome glanced back at Eva, bewildered. Eva ran to catch up and grabbed Salome's arm.

"Come on," she growled. "I want to know what's going on."

The two girls hurried up the stairwell after Sarah and Salif; Salome caught her breath as the outer door opened and the wind struck her face. But she ducked and ran on after them. Already the rotors of the helicopter were turning slowly, as if some remote command had reached it before Salif did. The pilot leaned out, beckoning Sarah with an imperious thumb.

"I don't get it," shouted Salome to Eva over the noise of rotors and wind. "Sarah's on our side."

"Whatever our side is," yelled Eva grimly. "Hey, Sarah! Wait!"

Sarah's hand was on the open hatch already, but she turned to crane past Salif as the two girls ran to her side. Salif turned to shout instructions to the pilot.

"What do you want, you two?" Sarah didn't raise her voice; her words were more for lipreading than for hearing.

"Eva. Your email!" Salome grabbed the printout from Eva's hands as she drew it from her pocket. "Sarah, can you look into this? We're not sure . . ."

Reluctantly, with a glance at the still-distracted Salif, Sarah peered down at the page. She hadn't had time to read further than the header, Salome was sure of it—but her face went pale.

<32>

Her head snapped up, and she glanced from Salome to Eva, thrusting the email back at the blonde girl. "Be careful!" she yelled, far more audibly this time.

Then Salif was back at Sarah's side, ushering her firmly up into the belly of the helicopter. Sarah slumped down into one of the seats, clicking on her seatbelt, but her eyes remained locked with Eva's.

The two girls watched as the helicopter rose into the air, then dipped and swooped away in the direction of the mainland. Eva scrunched the email printout between her fingers. Salif, without another word, slouched back toward the stairwell and disappeared.

There was sudden silence, but for the moan of the wind in the rocks.

"What was that?" Salome spread her hands.

"I don't know," said Eva. "But I did not like the sound of it."

Together they followed Salif's path back toward the stairwell. "She knew something," muttered Salome.

"But didn't have time to tell us what," said Eva bitterly. "And I'm no further ahead at making a decision. Should I follow up on this or not? 'Be careful.' Well, I was going to do that anyway!" She stuffed the printout back in her pocket. "Thanks a million, Sarah Lopez."

"I think I want to walk around outdoors for a bit," said Salome, hesitating at the stairwell door. "I need to think."

"Funny how that's so much easier outside of the Center, yes?" Eva gave her a dry look.

There was barely more than two square miles of surface, but it was always just enough to feel free of the Center, thought Salome as they trudged headlong into the wind, each girl wrapped in her own thoughts.

Or that was usually the case, since one was usually alone. Today, of course, it had to be different. Not far ahead, she could

<33>

make out the shapes of the Project Husky patrol moving swiftly toward them. They both came to a halt.

"Dang," said Eva softly. "Can't even get any peace out here."

The sleds were running on wheels, bumping less than smoothly along the sparse and bare vegetation; the robotic huskies lurched along, dragging them over rock and tussock with an understandable lack of concern for the human passengers on the sleds. It struck Salome that the students on the experimental ride looked thoroughly shaken, and she couldn't help grinning.

As they drew rapidly closer, though, her smile faded. The students didn't look just shaken; they looked downright traumatized. Dmitri Vasiliev, a Ukrainian boy with white-blond hair, gave a hoarse yell and punched at the screen of his phone; jerkily, the robots drew to a halt. Despite their crude mechanical appearance, Salome half expected them to pant. Dmitri himself was gasping for breath.

"What's up?" she called. "What happened?"

Eva took a step forward and scanned the sleds. "And where's Slack?"

"Slack?" Dmitri flopped forward over the front of the sled, looking exhausted. "In the infirmary."

"He's what?" exclaimed Salome.

"Yeah." Dmitri stretched his arms as if they were aching. "This is such a small island and flat. You wouldn't imagine it had so many bumps."

"And crevices," put in Abiona Okafor. "And cliff edges." She shoved her wind-tossed black hair out of her face. "That's what happened to Slack. Amazingly, these so-called huskies think they can take a forty-degree slope at full speed without any harm. Well, they can. But the humans aboard? Not so resilient."

<34>

Salome gasped. "Oh, poor Slack!"

"He's all right," said Abiona. "Bruises mostly—nothing broken, I *think*. But I feel like breaking these creatures." She threw a scrunched-up bit of paper at the robots.

"A bit expensive to break," observed Dmitri. "But they definitely need to go back to the lab for more testing." He turned to yell at the sled behind. "Right, Adam and Leo?"

The two boys behind gave sullen grunts of agreement.

"We have to go see Slack," said Salome.

"Good luck upgrading those brutes," called Eva with a smile.

With a quick farewell to the husky teams, the two girls hurried to the main surface stairwell and made their way to the Center's clinical wing.

Slack, huddled under a fleece blanket in an infirmary bed, looked thoroughly sorry for himself. His eyes, raised miserably to meet them as they entered, were the eyes of a whipped puppy.

"Oh, come on, Slack." Salome sat on the edge of his bed and patted his arm. "Abiona says you didn't break anything."

"Abiona's wrong," said Slack morosely. "I broke my tailbone. And I can't do anything about it except suffer till it heals."

Eva put her hand over her mouth, stifling giggles. Salome, too, found herself tempted to laugh, but she shot the Russian girl a warning look and mouthed, *Poor Slack!*

"What's so funny?" complained Slack. "It hurts."

"I bet it does," spluttered Eva. "It's ironic, that's all. The huskies don't have tails to break. But it turns out you do!"

<35>

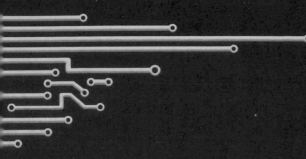

Five

—This was your best idea, Salome 👏👏👏, said Eva seriously.
—And you have had some good ones. I applaud you 🙌🎓.

Salome glanced sideways at Eva, blushing a little with pleasure.

—Don't speak too soon, Eva. It hasn't actually worked yet!

—It's working just fine. **Eva's brow furrowed slightly.** —Just because we have not begun the real project about . . . 🐛🐟🐢🐠 🐻⚪⚪⚫🌱✂️🌿

—Careful! **Salome warned her.** —We don't know whether this system is hackable!

—They all are. **Eva gave her friend a mischievous grin.** —But 👶💻💾👩💻👶💻 will need more ✂️ than we are going to give them . . .

—What's ✂️?

—It's thyme. Get it? Oh, wait, no. Wait. Ah! I mean 🕐. They will need more 🕐 than we will give them.

Salome laughed out loud. —How are you even making pictures in my head?

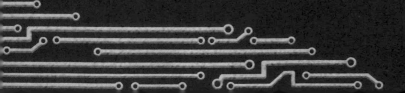

—Pictures? Oh, you mean these? **Eva gave her a smirk.** — 🐼
🏭 🐦 👻 😺

—Eva Vygotsky, stop fooling around and listen . . . I think
I have a contact!

Eva turned, her eyes wide. "Really?" she asked.

Salome tapped the tiny device behind her ear. "MindReader
only, please," she said sternly.

"I don't have the patience! Tell me."

Salome sat forward, cross-legged on her yoga mat. "Her name
is Ana, and she's a student at the Ma'yaarr Complex. And . . ." She
trailed off and shrugged. "And that's pretty much all I know . . .
except that what Mikael said at the assembly was true—that every
Center student has been given a MindReader device. Including
Ana!"

"You already spoke to her on it?" There was a touch of disappointment in Eva's voice.

"No, I talked to her on a message board on the Center
intranet," admitted Salome. "But *now* we're going to MindReader
her, together! Or we're going to try . . ."

Eva nodded. "Good idea."

—I want to make it a conference call, **said Salome.** —I think
we'll get a better . . . well, a better signal . . . if we do it together.

—Together. **Eva grinned.** — 👭

<<>>

—You've got to come! **enthused Ana.** —I promise you there's
nothing to be nervous about. Ma'yaarr is the best Center and the
best place in the world!

—Is that so? For real? **Eva winked at Salome.** —Why don't you
show us, then? Prove it!

There was such a long silence at the other end of the line that Salome felt nervousness fluttering in her stomach. It wasn't that she didn't trust this Ana; everything she'd said both in their traditional messages and in this MindReader session had been open, enthusiastic, and forthright. Yes, of course there were disadvantages. No shops for thousands of miles! Some of the students were annoying—of course they were! Weren't there always a few in every school?

Ana, decided Salome, sounded like a Ma'yaarr version of herself. She couldn't be a Ma'yaarr version of Eva, thought Salome with amusement, because Eva Vygotsky was a one-off. But otherwise Ana could have been a student at any one of the worldwide Centers, and one who fit right in. And with the MindReader at play, Salome was far more willing to put her faith in Ana than in whoever had written that email to Eva. An official heading didn't make it a genuine FBI communication, did it? With MindReader, at least she could trust Ana.

But she also needed Ana to trust *them*. And, now, for nearly three minutes—no, 3:28—she had vanished into the ether.

Salome cleared her throat. She turned to Eva in disappointment. "I think we lost her."

"Wait." Eva's eyes narrowed.

There was a tickle behind Salome's ear, a featherlight vibration that increased almost to a buzz, like static on an ancient landline.

Then Eva turned to her with a dazzling smile. Salome didn't have time to wonder: a fraction of a second later, the message reached her.

—🐿🐢🐊🐟🐢🐛🐞🐚🐌🐓

—🌳🌳🌳🌳🌳🌳🌿🌱🌹🌸🌺

<38>

— OK

Eva gave a squeal of delighted laughter; she was usually so reserved that Salome was taken aback. "This Ana—she's my soul mate! Visuals are very much more straightforward!" Eva lightly tapped the MindReader behind her ear and sent a single image into the conversation.

— ➡ SOON

Ana's electronic telepathy bubbled with delight in Salome's head. —You're going to come? I'm so happy! I'll be waiting to welcome you, friend! So long, until we meet in Ma'yaarr!

Eva peeled off her MindReader and tossed it to the yoga mat. "Salome, this place sounds—no, it *looks* wonderful! So we'll go to Ma'yaarr then, yes?"

Salome had promised herself she'd be cool and collected, that she'd treat the decision with clinical detachment and a thorough risk assessment. But right now, all she could think about was what she was going to pack.

"Of course we are, Eva. I think the whole Ghost Network will want to come, even John." Salome gave a squeal of excitement and reached to clutch her friend's hands. "We're going to find your parents!"

The Ghost Network—or most of them, gathered in John and Slack's dorm room—were every bit as excited as Salome had hoped they would be. Akane sat cross-legged on Slack's bed, scrolling on her phone screen through a list of excursion opportunities in the Amazon. In Slack's absence, Eva was flicking idly through his collection of frankly garish Bermuda shirts. Even John looked more cheerful than he had in days. He was reading

<39>

and rereading Eva's email printout, alternately frowning and nodding in approval.

Salome could bear the suspense no longer. "Even emo John Laine, then?" she prodded eagerly. "You're going to come along?"

John gave her a dark look but then grinned. "All right, I know I've been a grouch lately. I had my reasons."

Still staring at her phone, Akane waved a dismissive arm. "Don't go into all that again. Just tell me you're coming with us, John. Because I am *not* missing this!" She brandished her phone under his nose. "Look! Kayaking, paddle boarding, high canopy walks . . . piranha fishing! Swimming with pink river dolphins!"

"So long as you're not dolphin fishing or swimming with piranhas," said John dryly, but his eyes gleamed with excitement. "But . . . look, it's just the reason behind the trip that's got me worried. This email . . . it's weird, don't you think? How would the FBI know about Eva's parents?"

"I don't know," said Salome, reaching out to squeeze Eva's hand. The Russian girl looked as cool and detached as ever, but she must have been freaking out at the prospect of finding her mother and father. And why would Sarah Lopez have warned them to *be careful* if she hadn't been sure it was all true?

Salome decided she didn't need to mention the alarm in the young journalist's eyes or the short time she'd had to give her urgent warning. "Sarah Lopez knew that email was real," Salome told John firmly. "She wanted us to be careful, but she seemed quite certain it wasn't a fraud."

"What did she say?" Akane glanced up.

"She had to leave," said Eva, shrugging. "Quickly. She didn't have time to explain. But she knew there was something to this."

<40>

Akane's brow furrowed. "That's not like Sarah. She's been really helpful before."

"Not her fault," said Salome quickly.

Akane arched a puzzled eyebrow. "How come?"

Taking a deep breath, Salome explained the scene outside Mikael's office, the argument, the hasty exchange at the helipad. "Your dad kind of lost it, John," she said guiltily. "I've never seen him like that. He was *furious* at something Sarah had done or something she'd said to him."

"He had Salif throw her straight off the island," confirmed Eva. "Well, fly her off it. In a helicopter. You know, he did not actually *throw* her."

"I don't understand." John looked more thoughtful than surprised, thought Salome. "This was after the assembly? It must have happened right after I saw her. And all she was doing was interviewing him for some backslapping Man of the Year thing in that *Alaskan Star* celeb rag. How could she have made him so mad, so fast?"

They stared at one another, perplexed.

"You know, I kinda don't care," said John at last. "If she was fighting with my dad, she had a good reason. I'm pretty sure if *I* started asking the right questions, he'd lose it."

"Or the wrong questions," mused Akane.

"Nobody wants to say it." John stood up. "Because I'm sitting right here. So I tell you what: *I'll say it.*" He took a breath. "I'm not sure we can trust my father. And neither are any of you."

Akane looked at the blanket on Slack's bed. Salome blushed. Eva glanced expectantly around them all.

<41>

"No," blurted Akane at last. "John, I know what you mean, and he's maybe got good reason for concealing something from us. He always does. But I *do* think there's something he isn't telling us."

"Same," whispered Salome. "Sorry, John."

"You don't have to apologize to me," said John. "I said it because I know it."

"But that means," said Akane slowly, "that we probably don't want him to know what we're planning. Even though the email says to consult him."

"I believe that email," said John, "but it doesn't mean I trust it or whoever wrote it. I think we need to make our own plans."

Akane rubbed her hands together. "Yes. We'll do what they suggest—but not the way they suggest it. How about it, Eva?"

Eva nodded. "I like this plan. I like it much better than the original. But how do we accomplish it?"

"We do," said John, "by setting up the ultimate prank on my dad." There was a light of bitter satisfaction in his eyes. "He'll never know what hit him."

"Oh, hang on," objected Salome. "Pull the wool over your dad's eyes? The guy who outsmarted Roy Lykos? I'm not sure that's even possible, John."

"Gotta agree," said Akane.

"Oh, you'll see." John grinned slyly. "Put it this way: I wasn't expelled from school in Fairbanks for picking my nose once too often. Leave the prank design to the master, guys."

Salome gazed around doubtfully at the others. "We did outwit Roy Lykos and escape from the Scarab's Temple," she said. "We might be ready to try this . . ."

<42>

"More than ready," said John confidently. "I know I can outwit my dad; I'm sure of it. And who's the only other real threat? Roy Lykos." He smiled. "And he's safely tucked away in San Quentin. "We're the Ghost Network, guys. Believe me—we've got this!"

<43>

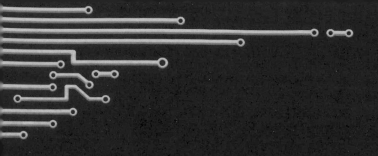

Six

How dare they . . .

Roy Lykos was not a man to display his emotions outwardly.
He was so far above the rest of the population, intellectually and
technologically, he could barely be described as simply human.
Why should he be controlled, then, by mere human emotions?

Yet inside him, the rage and resentment seethed every bit as
wildly as he imagined it had for Stone Age man.

His cell was sweltering and far too small for his liking. This
prison was infamous for both its inmates and its high security;
it was one of the drawbacks of the state penitentiary he'd been
assigned. He hated being here—he hated being in any sort of
captivity. He was not a normal criminal or prisoner. What was
the court thinking, to confine a mind like his? How could they
possibly understand the stratospheric heights of his plans or
ambitions?

And what had his high-echelon friends been thinking when
they turned their backs on him and had dissociated themselves?
That was something they would certainly pay for, later. Roy Lykos's

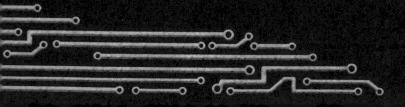

mind was far too vast and all-consuming to allow him to forget any kind of betrayal.

However, in some ways, San Quentin was not as bad as he had feared. Roy smiled wryly to himself. It turned out that many of the nation's most notorious, dangerous, and violent criminals—with whom he was not associated—were big consumers of technology. The inmates were as inclined as the general population to revere those who created and brought tech to them; Roy was twice the celebrity in here that he had been in the outside world.

He of all people knew the value of contacts, and here he was making new, highly beneficial ones every day. New contacts with far less scruples. Roy Lykos had never wasted time or opportunities, and he was not about to start now. His growing network was what kept him sane: knowing that every day, every conversation, every favor he granted brought him closer to revenge.

The people whom he shared his captivity with were highly useful. However, the person who could help him the most was free and as loose in the world as a lethal airborne virus. Roy laughed softly to himself. Yes, retribution would come soon, with his ally's assistance. It pained him to rely on someone so unstable, so potentially explosive, but his needs must be met. Instability could, after all, have spectacular and entertaining results.

Mikael Laine and his brattish son would pay for what they'd done to him. Roy knew that with a clinical certainty.

Perhaps not entirely clinical, though. . . . There were moments when he positively thirsted for their blood. That was a human reflex, he didn't doubt. But then, sometimes, human desires had their place. Roy closed his eyes, breathed deeply, and prepared

<45>

himself for proper meditation. He'd learned to train himself to achieve calmness and serenity through the bloodiest of revenge fantasies, and he was looking forward to this one . . .

A brisk clacking on the cell door interrupted him. His eyes snapped open, and he barked: "Wha . . . ?"

But the door had swung open before the word had completely come out of his mouth. This was yet another irritation: the lack of respect from staff, even the ones he'd bribed. For this, too, there would be retaliation. Eventually. Right now, he found himself glaring at the prison guard.

"You've got a visitor, Mr. Lykos. And apparently the visiting area isn't suitable." The guard sniffed, barely audibly, as a shadowy figure stepped forward.

Roy did not rise. He smiled at his visitor. "Well, now. This is a pleasant surprise."

"Good day, Mr. Lykos. You already know what a big fan I am of your work . . ."

<46>

Seven

"What do you mean, you can't come?" Salome stared at Akane, aghast. John gave a groan of disappointment.

"I'm as upset about it as you are," moaned Akane. She punched Slack's mattress, and he winced. "Sorry, Slack."

"You didn't hurt me," he said warily, eyeing her clenched fist. "But watch what you're doing there. I'm still broken, you know."

Salome patted his hand. "You'll be better in no time. We all want you to come to the Amazon too, Slack. And Akane, you absolutely *have* to come!"

"I can't!" Akane cried. "You know I want to, Salome. But I told you about the message I got this morning? My grandmother's ill, really ill this time, and I can't go off-grid. The Ma'yaarr Complex is miles from anywhere, and what if communication breaks down? What if I can't leave on short notice to get to her? At least staying here I know I can get a helicopter out really fast."

"And there's no way my bone's gonna recover *that* quickly," said Slack firmly. "I'll have to support you guys from this hospital bed—or from that soft beanbag chair they've given me to sit on at best."

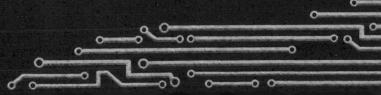

"Oh, Akane, that's terrible luck." Salome clenched her jaw; she could see Akane's dilemma, and it was barely a choice at all. Salome wished that Akane's friend's parents hadn't sent that message today of all days. However, some things, Salome told herself inwardly and firmly, were just more important. "But we'll miss you so much. The team's going to be lost without you."

Akane shook her head. "No, you won't. I wish, I *so* wish I was coming—swimming with river dolphins!—but I can't. Like Slack says, we'll be your contacts here."

"Yeah." Slack's eyes were surprisingly bright, and his expression was quite cheerful. "And look on the positive side, Akane. The two of us will get to know each other better."

Akane rolled her eyes. "I think we know each other pretty well already, Slack." But she smiled down at him.

"You know, it's not the worst idea," said John slowly. "It could be useful to have a remote team, monitoring us from the outside. In case anything happens."

"Nothing's going to happen," said Salome. "Ana's going to look out for us when we get there, and the complex looks amazing."

"Something's happened both the other times we've left the complex," John pointed out.

"But this is nothing more than a quest to find Eva's parents. It's a bit of a mystery," insisted Salome, "but there's nothing sinister about it."

"Sarah Lopez might beg to differ," said Akane darkly.

"Her reaction could have been related to anything," declared Salome. "For all we know, she might have just been worried about how Eva and her parents will get along! It's not like we had time to talk to her properly."

<48>

"Just be careful." Slack glanced from Salome to John. "And let Akane and me know if there's any sign of trouble."

"I promise," sighed Salome. "But I still wish you guys were coming with us."

"Me too," said Akane mournfully.

"We still don't know how we're getting to the Ma'yaarr Complex," Salome reminded them, with a hopeful glance at John. "The official way isn't an option. Any developments with this 'prank' of yours?"

"There might be, by now." John grinned. "Mom's visiting the school this evening—she and Dad and I are having dinner together in his office. A nice family chat." His smile became wicked.

"By then I'm hoping Dad'll have heard some, um . . . some good news."

"It's going to be a really good opportunity to promote the school to potential new candidates!" Mikael was in full excited mode over the grilled sea bass, and John had no intention of interrupting him. "A lot of the people attending this conference are going to be high-tech business executives. And our old colleague Yasuo Yamamoto is out of the picture and facing his own federal investigation for enabling Lykos and funding him. So the Center is going to need new sources of funding—and this is exactly the chance I've been waiting for! Keynote speaker, no less."

"You be careful in Shanghai," warned Tina, setting down her fork. "You don't know where Roy Lykos still has operatives, Mikael. He's still got a lot of personal loyalty with some pretty

<49>

shady government people. And you know China's going to be looking for a way to connect with you and your technology."

"I'm fully aware of that, and I'll see it coming," he reassured her. "I've got my own Chinese contacts, and they're not all beholden to the government—whatever the government thinks." He laughed. "Believe me, Tina, this is a really exciting opportunity. And I can take advantage of the trip to visit the Center in Zhejiang province. It's only about four hours' journey from Shanghai."

"I think it's gonna be great, Mom," said John. "Don't worry—Dad can handle it. You should see the way he holds an audience captive. He'll come back with about ten new sponsors, I betcha—" He couldn't keep a straight face any longer and had to clamp his mouth shut over a forkful of sea bass.

Oh, it was going to be a great imaginary conference. Zhou Zhou, their former fellow student at the Scarab's Temple, knew just how to make an enticing online brochure—and he was very good at finding the right names to headline an international tech event in China. Even John almost believed the lineup when a copy of the slick invitation dropped into his inbox. The conference sounded exactly like the kind of event where his father should be promoting the Centers, raising funds for scholarships, and recruiting potential new wealthy students.

It was a pity the Shanghai Convention for Technical Education existed only in the minds of himself, Slack, and Zhou. But wasn't this what his dad had wanted all along—a resourceful son who could create complex projects out of nothing but code? John suppressed another snicker.

<50>

Mikael shot him a surprised glance, and John turned his laughter into a polite cough.

"So when do you leave, Dad?" he asked.

"Day after tomorrow," said Mikael. "Seems I'm a replacement speaker for someone who couldn't make it, but I'm not complaining! There's going to be a lot to organize."

"I can help with your keynote speech, if you like," offered John.

Mikael's eyebrows shot up, but he smiled and nodded. "That would be great, John! I'm in need of some slightly more up-to-date jokes, am I right?"

"You bet," grinned John.

A twinge of guilt rippled through his stomach. His father's eyes were warm and grateful, and his mother looked genuinely delighted that the frosty atmosphere between the two had dissipated.

Still, John wasn't about to tell him the truth—not now. When his father found out about the deception he'd created, that would be soon enough to feel guilty and accept his punishment. Getting him, Salome, and Eva off this island was way more important than his father's trust, at least for right now. The rest would have to be rebuilt over time.

And it wasn't like Mikael didn't deserve a little betrayal after everything he'd put him and his mom through. John widened his smile, suppressing a glimmer of remorse.

<>>

—Dad's getting Howard McAuliffe to fill in for his teaching commitments, John told Zhou, with a conspiratorial grin toward Slack.

—Can't say I'll be sorry to miss those lectures!

<51>

He and Slack were sprawled on their beds, MindReaders installed behind their ears. It was almost like having a private conversation with Slack, except for the dry, amused, and emoji-free responses from the other side of the world. Zhou's voice was as clear and precise as it had always been; it felt like there was some kind of invisible ghost in the room.

—McAuliffe probably won't even notice you're missing, indicated Zhou.

—John says Mikael fell for it completely, grinned Slack. —Great work on that invitation and the website, Zhou!

—Yeah, said John, shaking off that ugly sense of guilt again. —We owe you one, Zhou Zhou.

—Oh, you owe me a lot more than one, pointed out Zhou wryly. —Who got you out of the Scarab's Temple before it exploded?

—Fair point, laughed Slack.

—We'll raise a tropical toast to you when we get there, Zhou. John winked at Slack, who groaned with regret and longing.

—Amazonas, Brazil, here we come!

<52>

Eight

The rear compartment of the military helicopter was horribly cramped and hot, but the worst part was the racket of the engine. By the time the rotors slowed and stopped, Salome was convinced she was deaf in one ear.

She signaled to John and Eva. *OK.*

The helicopter crew had almost completed their landing routine. She could hear them now, laughing and chatting as they strode away across the landing pad.

"Anchorage." Salome risked saying it out loud, and her voice sounded strange and echoey in her ears. "We made it."

Eva wriggled in her cramped space and began to elbow the metal panel between them and the cargo bay. "I can't wait to get out of here," she muttered.

"Worst flight ever," growled John, trying to stretch his shoulders. "But I'm glad we did it. Dad had no idea we were here the whole time. He must be nearly at the gate for his flight to Chicago by now. Eva, you can hit that panel harder. Nobody's around anymore."

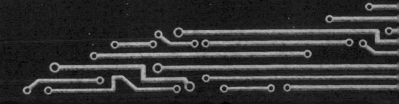

Eva shot him a resentful glance, but she was the only one of them who could reach it in the cramped space. Taking a deep breath, she slammed her arm against the panel one last time, and it popped out with a resounding clang. Fresh cold air flooded the compartment, and all three gasped at once.

"Oh, that's lovely," moaned Salome. She wriggled out after Eva and stood up, stretching her muscles.

"I think both my legs have fallen asleep," complained John.

Salome dragged him out by his ankles, and he rolled out, then staggered to his feet. "Your dad really was excited about this conference," Salome remarked. "I feel kind of bad."

"Don't. If he wasn't so self-obsessed, he might've actually noticed three stowaways in the supply chopper." John rolled his eyes.

"The flight from Chicago to Shanghai is nearly twenty hours with connections," said Eva. "We've got plenty of time to disappear before he realizes what's happened."

"Yes, but from here to Manaus is going to take nearly a day, with the connections," pointed out Salome anxiously. "If he guesses we're on our way to Brazil—"

"He won't," John flatly assured her. "He has no idea about what we have planned. Like I said: self-obsessed. He'll probably have assumed all along that Eva would come straight to him to arrange any trip to the Ma'yaarr Complex. Once he catches on, he'll know we're gone, but he won't know where. Zhou booked the flights, and I think he must've pinged the booking requests at least twice around the world to hide their origins. Even Dad won't trace the source quickly."

<54>

"We've got two hours to get to the gate," said Eva, "but that doesn't mean we should hang around. Grab your bags. Let's go!"

<<>>

Was there anything worse than waiting in airports? Salome sighed quietly and stared at her phone screen. Oh well: with diplomats for parents, she was used to it. But her experiences had drained the glamour of air travel, especially when it didn't involve first-class lounges.

Eva sat opposite her, fidgeting uncomfortably on a lumpy plastic seat. John lay sprawled beside Salome across three chairs, his head on an armrest. She had a feeling he'd fallen asleep, but she couldn't be bothered to check. She could feel her own eyelids beginning to grow heavy.

Her boredom immediately vanished as a notification popped up on her phone screen. Salome frowned. It was from the encrypted message service that Sarah Lopez had always used to communicate with the Ghost Network. Suddenly fully awake, Salome sat forward and thumbed her screen.

Hey, Sarah! What's up?

That email of Eva's. I've had a poke around. I was able to find out a few things.

Salome took a sharp breath. Eva glanced up with curiosity, but then she returned to her own phone. Salome tapped urgently at the keyboard on her screen.

What is it, Sarah?

Sorry, am in a hurry, can't chat. Shouldn't tell you this, really. It may be a good story and I should be keeping it to myself for now, but I'm worried about you three. And you've done a lot for me. But I gotta be quick.

Go on, typed Salome. **Won't interrupt, I promise.**

OK.

Sarah was typing . . .

[. . .]

[. . .]

Sarah was typing for quite a long time, thought Salome as her uneasy feelings continued to increase.

Her phone blipped, and the message that appeared filled the entire screen and more.

I haven't been able to find out much about the Ma'yaarr Complex, so this is vague. What I do know is that there are rumors one of the worldwide Centers has gone rogue. Trouble is they're all so secretive it's almost impossible to know which one has gone completely off the grid. Mikael's keeping it quiet, and he did NOT like that I'd found out enough to ask him about what's happened and where. That's why I got thrown out of the Wolf's Den. I'm sure he's panicking, doesn't know how to deal. But the rumor is the students may have taken over the running of the—

Salome couldn't help herself. **WHAT.**

Said you wouldn't interrupt. It's being run by students.

The message was complete. Salome hesitated, then risked asking a question. **But Eva's parents? What's that about?**

Don't know. But a couple has been reported missing in the Amazonas region, near where the Ma'yaarr is located. Were on a tourist expedition, wandered off on their own, possibly deliberately. Haven't been seen for days. Could be Eva's parents—in which case there's no way for me to know what happened to them after they made contact with

<56>

the Center. IF the Ma'yaarr is the rogue Center. And IF they made contact there and IF they didn't get eaten by jaguars.

Ha ha, butted in Salome, but she felt a shiver surge down her spine.

Yeah, it's not good, Salome. Mikael didn't know about the missing pair. Seemed shocked when I confronted him, tried to say it was nothing to do with Ma'yaarr. Maybe he's right. But maybe it's best you stay out of Brazil till I can find out more. I don't think he'd want you going there, whatever you heard from the FBI.

Salome sucked in a big breath. But Eva wants to find her parents. She NEEDS to.

Doesn't matter. Too dangerous, Salome, or I think so. For now. Wait till I know more. I gotta go. Bye xx

Wait, Sarah.

Sarah?

Sarah, are you there?

Sarah, it seemed, was no longer typing.

Salome lowered her phone, her heart pounding. She stared at Eva, who was now engrossed in some word game. The Russian girl muttered a curse, then gave a short laugh, and filled in another series of letters. Salome's heart wrenched. How would Eva react if Salome told her that her mother and father were missing, perhaps dead—and that may have happened because they were looking for her?

No, thought Salome. *No, I'm not going to tell her. Or John. Not yet.*

Eva wanted so badly to find her parents, and from what Sarah had told her, Salome was more certain than ever that the missing

<57>

couple were the Vygotskys. Eva seemed to be their friend, but it struck Salome again how little they knew about her—or her erratic, AI-given abilities. If Eva discovered her parents were in danger, who knew how she might react? What she might *do*?

We're the Ghost Network, thought Salome, *or three of them, anyway. Because Eva counts. And this is Ghost Network business now.*

A rogue Center—one that Mikael was desperate to hide—was definitely part of their mission. Salome set her jaw sternly.

It doesn't matter what Sarah thinks—or Mikael, for that matter. The Ghost Network looks after its own.

<58>

Nine

"*Bozhe moi,* I hate flying." Eva's face was twisted into a scowl as she grabbed her bag from the overhead compartment. "I haven't ever flown much, and already I know this much. It's way worse than the Siberian railways. A thousand times worse."

They edged and stumbled along the aisle and out of the plane, their small bags bumping awkwardly against seats and some lingering passengers.

"In defense of a vital industry," said John solemnly, "flights are not always that long, and there're usually a lot fewer connections."

"This was enough," Eva declared firmly. "Flying—what's the thing you say? It sucks. *And* it is bad for the climate. So it *totally* sucks."

Salome managed to laugh. "I've done way more flying than you, Eva, and I happen to agree with every word you said. But at least we made that carbon offset donation."

"Huh," Eva snorted. "It's like buying indulgences from the Pope."

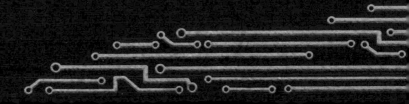

"What about flying with my dad from Little Diomede to Morocco?" John nudged Eva with his elbow.

"That was *fun*," protested Eva. "And it was necessary to save you. And it didn't involve hanging around in departure lounges. We just *went*."

"Not how it usually works, I'm afraid. That's my dad's do-as-I-like privilege again." As they traipsed down the plane steps, John puffed out a sigh of relief. The air was clammier and hotter than it had been in Miami. "Now we just have to find the Ma'yaarr Complex. Can't imagine that'll be straightforward."

"Ana's on the message board, and she'll guide us," said Salome. "It'll be easier than you think."

It was even easier than Salome had predicted, because just beyond passport control, they found their way partly obstructed by two suited men who stepped forward in the arrivals area. John came to a surprised halt; neither of them was holding a board with their names written on it.

"Not us," he began. "I think you're looking for somebody—"

"Somebody else? No, you're Mr. Laine. And these two are Ms. Vygotsky and Ms. Abraham."

The taller man was not asking them a question; he was stating the facts. John felt a chill of unease as he stared at his mirrored sunglasses. After a long pause, the man removed them.

"I'm Agent Baeker; my colleague here is Agent Field."

"*Agent?*" Eva stiffened.

"FBI?" Salome narrowed her eyes suspiciously.

Agent Baeker removed his ID from an inside pocket and flashed it briefly in her face. "Of course. We're here to escort you to the Ma'yaarr Complex; it's quite a journey. Please follow us."

<60>

John was too dumbstruck to argue. As the three reluctantly followed the agents, neither of whom had offered to carry their bags, he elbowed Salome surreptitiously.

"We're here incognito," he hissed. "We didn't take the FBI option."

"Something's gone wrong," whispered Eva. Her eyes narrowed with suspicion; she had never trusted bureaucrats and government officials, John remembered—not since she'd been swept off a Siberian train by them and ferried to his father.

"I don't understand," he admitted.

"I don't like it," muttered Salome. "How could they have known? Your father?"

"No," said John quietly. "I may not trust my dad, but I know him pretty well. He had no idea what we were planning. Whatever this is, it's not official."

Out in the scorching sunlight, the two men led them toward a car parked in the limo waiting zone. Wiping sweat from his eyes, John stared at them.

"Besides the obvious question of who sent them," he muttered to Salome, "just look at them. You'd think they'd at least take their jackets off."

"They're like automatons," she agreed. "And they're not even looking back to make sure that we're following. That doesn't unnerve me; it just really, *really* annoys me. They're just certain we'll follow like good little students." She made a growling noise in her throat.

Eva, though, halted suddenly and turned to them both. "It's OK!" She tapped her MindReader behind her ear. "Ana's just messaged me. Well, that was an understatement. Since we came

<61>

out of the airport building, it's been an emoji-fest!" She smirked. "Pictures are more direct; they mean more than words. Ana knows this as well as I do. Well, she knows about these men, and she is waiting for us. And I have messages coming in from other students. They are all so eager to meet us!"

Salome's frown melted into a grin of relief. She reached for her own device and tapped it with a fingertip. "John, turn yours on. I'll introduce you to our friend Ana!"

In a matter of seconds, the MindReader session turned into an excited group chat session. John barely had time to say a nervous hello to Ana before his brain was deluged with happy greeting emojis.

—WELCOME TO BRAZIL! 💚🌳🌴🌲🌺🐢🐵🙌🤚 ✋✋✋ We can't wait to meet you!!! So happy you have come! Go with the drivers, they're all good! So happy to have you here with us, Eva and Salome, and so excited to meet you, John Laine! See you soon!!! 🐢🐢🐢🐢🐢🐢🐢

There wasn't really time to respond beyond an awkward —Hi back!! ✋, so John was content to let himself be swept along with Eva's unusual cheerfulness and Salome's enthusiasm. The sleek black car was at least air-conditioned, and even with the two agents riding in front, there was plenty of space on the leather seats in the rear. Because John was sitting between Salome and Eva, he had to crane his neck past them to catch a glimpse of the city. For the supposed gateway to the rain forest, it was far more built up and developed than he had expected. Dense, cheaply constructed housing shared the city's space with monuments, elegant European-style nineteenth-century mansions, and twenty-first-century skyscrapers. A vast river came into view, and John

<62>

saw suspension bridges along with cargo freighters thronging a busy port.

"Crossing the Rio Negro now." Agent Baeker craned over his seat to update them after a long silence. "You'll be right in the Amazonian forest soon."

"We're driving into the jungle?" Salome raised her eyebrows.

"No. We'll pick up a boat shortly. You'll see the meeting of the Negro and the Solimoes river; that's where the Amazon forms, and that's where we leave the car." A rare and swift grin flitted across Baeker's features. "The boat will not be air-conditioned, so enjoy the cool air for now."

It might not have been air-conditioned, but the inflatable boat was a smoother and more comfortable ride than John had expected. As it purred up the slow green waters, the noise of birds and insects grew steadily louder, shriller, and more all-encompassing. Agent Baeker left the side of the silent Agent Field and parked himself next to them, holding a state-of-the-art tablet in his hands. He tapped and swiped, the reflection of both the water and the screen rippling on his impassive face.

"Your clothing sizes, Ms. Abraham?" he asked Salome. "Head size down to foot size, please. You will be expected to wear the Center's approved attire during your stay." Catching sight of her face, he twisted his mouth. "Don't look so alarmed. It's casual but standardized."

It was the first of many questions he asked each of them in turn, brusque and curt. PC, Mac, or Linux? Food allergies and preferences? Sporting interests? Conventional bedroom, hammock, or tree house?

<63>

John felt hoarse by the time his own interrogation was over, and he turned to Salome with a face of amused relief. "We never got anything like this in the helicopter on the way to the Wolf's Den."

She smiled. "I guess it's good that they want to make us feel at home. And the 'uniform' doesn't sound too intimidating—shorts or cropped jeans, T-shirts or tank tops, flip-flops or Converse, as far as I can make out. It's not like they're making us wear kilts and loafers." She laughed, glancing at Agent Baeker, but he didn't react in the slightest.

"I'm kind of impressed," admitted John. "I asked for Linux—guess you did too. And I went for a tree house for accommodation."

"Same here," agreed Salome. "I like the sound of this place, John."

"I think I like it a lot." John glanced at Eva, who was answering Baeker's questions with her old monosyllabic wariness. "The climate sure beats the one at the Wolf's Den." He paused, thoughtfully. "You know . . . maybe it's time we started doing our own thing, Salome. All the Centers teach the same curriculum, don't they? If it's as good as it sounds—what's to stop us from staying here longer?"

"Forever?" Salome sounded astonished.

"For our school careers," John corrected her. "Though, who knows?" He lowered his voice. "And to be honest, I quite like the idea of one without teachers."

"Hey. Speak for yourself. I want my qualifications."

"Me too. But if the students here are smart enough to learn on their own, we are too. Come on, Salome—my dad doesn't really

<64>

get me; he never has. For all his messing with our heads, he doesn't get *any* of us. And we've had a heck of a lot of real-world experience."

Salome blinked at him. She still looked shocked, but he knew she was turning it over in her mind the same way he was.

"I'm serious, Salome. Look at this place." John gestured around the rain forest that flourished along the riverbanks; the canopy and the underbrush were alive with birdsong, insect chatter, and the shrieks and hoots of unseen animals. "It's paradise. You could call it a sort of graduation.

"We're the Ghost Network—and maybe it's time to leave . . . our *collective* father behind."

"I really don't like these guys," whispered Salome to John as the boat purred gently down the broad green river.

Agent Baeker and Agent Field had not exactly been chatty on day one of the river journey, but now they had stopped talking to Salome, Eva, and John altogether. They sat side by side at the front of the boat, not bothering to glance back—the same way they had behaved on the walk from the airport building. The two men were clearly confident that the three students would obey and follow without question.

"I know exactly what you mean," he told Salome in a low voice.

"Maybe it's just their nature," she said. "I mean, they're FBI agents. They're probably trained to be completely impassive."

"They're FBI agents *as far as we know*," growled Eva on John's other side. "I bet I could fake an ID at least as good as theirs."

"Oh no, Eva," protested Salome. "I'm sure they're for real. Just not very friendly."

<65>

"I'm not." Eva glared at the men's spines.

"I've got to admit," whispered John, "I'm increasingly feeling more like Eva on this."

The three lapsed into silence, watching the water drift by, laced with a silvery morning mist. The sun was only just rising over the rain forest on the banks, its rays making the boat's wake glitter. The previous night's camp had been basic but comfortable—but John had barely been able to sleep. He hadn't liked the way the agents took turns playing sentry; they hadn't seemed to watch the forest or the black nighttime river at all. John had gotten the feeling that an anaconda could slither into camp unchallenged, because Baeker and Field had seemed interested only in keeping an eye on their three charges.

The day passed slowly. As beautiful as the river was, John's unease was growing. The agents spoke only to offer them food, but it wasn't just their unfriendliness that bothered him—it was their constant surreptitious glances. Now and again they would mutter to each other, but John couldn't make out a word they were saying. By the time the sun had sunk in the deep-blue sky and was gilding the treetops with a radiant orange glow, John was feeling downright antsy about spending another night in the forest with them.

Twilight had set in by the time the boat slowed and drifted against a wooden jetty in what looked like an unused boatyard. The air was cooler, a misty blue-gray, and the nighttime insects were in full, noisy chorus. John held out his arms as Baeker unloaded the boat and took one of the two-man tents from him. Baeker, too surprised to react, let him take it.

"We'll help with these tonight," said John with a bright smile.

<66>

Baeker hesitated and then, with a glance at Field, nodded. John hurried over to Salome and Eva, and they began to unpack the nylon tent.

"You two deal with the tent," murmured Eva. "I'm going to go over there and look at the river."

It wasn't like her to shirk a job, and John's eyebrows shot up, but he smiled as he watched her wander innocently over to the agents' vicinity. Eva had ears like a bat. It was one of the unintentional by-products of her prototype inner AI, though—since she took her superhuman hearing for granted—it seemed to be an enhancement of a thoroughly natural talent. If there was anything to be discovered, Eva would hear it without Baeker and Field even realizing she was listening.

Eva sat on the bank, rested her arms on her knees, and gazed out at the water's silvery twilight surface. John imagined her ears swiveling like a radar so clearly that he could almost see it happen, and he grinned to himself.

It wasn't any trouble to set up the tent, so they didn't really miss Eva's help, but the interior ground cover had to be secured down. John unfolded it and beckoned Salome, and they crawled into the tent with it together, exchanging a conspiratorial grin.

"I'm starting to come around to your and Eva's point of view," whispered Salome as she attached one corner securely. "I don't trust these guys one bit. I watched them all day, and I didn't like how they were staring at us when they thought we weren't looking."

"Once you notice, you can't unsee it," murmured John.

There was a rustle at the tent's opening, and Eva elbow-crawled in beside them. Her eyes shone with angry excitement.

<67>

"What did you hear?" hissed John. "I know that's what you were up to!"

"Mostly," said Eva, "they just complained about this whole mission. They do not like us any more than we like them; I can tell you that much." She gave a dry grin. "But it seems that's because they don't see the point of it. They're under orders, and they don't even know what it's all about." She hesitated, and her face darkened with anger. "Then I heard them talking about the missing couple—my parents."

"We don't know for sure they're your parents," whispered Salome gently.

"I do," Eva told her with a glare. "No doubt—do you understand? And these men, they called my mother and father 'two idiot middle-aged rich dopes who thought they knew better than their tour guide.'"

John whistled softly. "So Baeker and Field have no idea at all," he said. "They don't know why your parents were searching for you."

"They might guess; they obviously know there's a connection, and that's why I'm here," said Eva. "But that's the extent of what they know."

Salome glanced at John. "So they're not here to help Eva find her parents. Why would they be assigned to us, then?"

"I think I know," declared Eva. "I think they're taking us deep into the jungle so that no one knows where we are and we lose phone contact. And then they will take us into government custody." She took a deep breath. "I think the US government wants complete control over the Ghost Network."

"Oh, no way," said John, alarmed.

<68>

"Not if we have anything to say about it," said Salome with a scowl. "We are an international group, and *I* am not even American!"

"Me neither," growled Eva. "I'm not really certain what I am but definitely not American."

"I *am*," pointed out John, "and I *still* don't want to be a tool of the state."

"So what do we do now?" asked Salome.

"We do what the Ghost Network always does," grinned John. "We fix this on our own. And from this point on, we make our own way to the Ma'yaarr Complex."

<69>

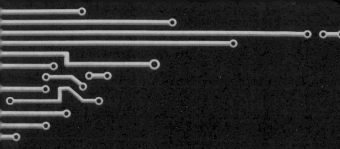

Ten

The glorious golden sunset had long faded, and the
chirping and trilling of poison dart frogs was slowly being overwhelmed by the scrape of cicadas and the scream of birds. Night
had finally settled over the camp. It was the blackest John had
ever seen; no moon rose above the forest canopy, and the stars
were obscured by thick foliage. He lay very still in his tent, trying
to listen for the sound of Baeker's and Field's breathing above the
noises of the forest, but it was impossible.

At last, he couldn't stand it any longer. As he tentatively unfas-
tened the tent flap and crawled out, his heart was in his mouth.
There was no movement from the agents' tent, and although he
couldn't make out any deep breathing or snoring noises, there
didn't seem to be any low voices in conversation.

Barefoot, he edged over to the tent that Salome and Eva
shared, feeling with his toes for brittle leaves or twigs that might
give him away. But just as he crouched to call softly to them,
their tent flap opened and both girls peered out.

"Are we good to go?" breathed Salome.

John nodded. "I think so. Be very quiet."

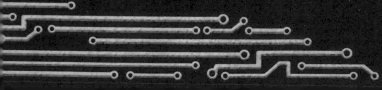

Like him, the girls had gone to bed fully dressed in shorts and T-shirts, but none of them put their sneakers on until they had crept a good distance from the camp. John was on pins and needles because he was afraid that Salome might step on a snake or a spider and wouldn't be able to stifle a shriek. But luck was with them, and they were able to get farther away without any incidents. With their shoes quickly back on their feet, they pressed on farther into the forest, John's phone glowing in his hand.

He risked raising his voice a little louder. "I wish Slack was here. He can navigate anywhere. He's clever." In a growl he added, "Way too clever."

"Don't be too envious, John." Eva growled. "It's not just his natural ability, after all. Your father's AI infusion improved his map-reading ability like crazy." Her voice became a little resentful. "He has that connection to the mother computer IIDA, just like the rest of you. She can help you with most things, yes?"

"You may not have the IIDA connection, Eva, but you're smart and instinctive enough not to need it," Salome reassured her. "That's what I believe. Anyway, John, don't worry about navigating; IIDA should be only for emergencies, and I don't want to communicate with her right now because it might get back to Mikael. With John's app we'll find the area well enough. And then with all our MindReaders, we'll let Ana guide us in. Um, how far do you think it is?"

"Only about ten miles," said John. "But we're in a rain forest, after all. The terrain is going to be rough."

"Let's aim back toward the river," suggested Eva.

"Jaguars and anacondas can swim, you know," said Salome with a shiver.

<71>

Eva shot her a glare. "That's not the point. So can piranhas."

Oh, great, thought John, with a roll of his eyes in the darkness. *Remind Salome about the piranhas, why don't you . . .*

"The point is," Eva went on, "it's easier to follow the river. Even with the app, we could lose our way in the dark—enough to add extra miles to the walk."

"Agreed," said John. "But Baeker and Field will be searching for us by daylight. We need to be ready to dive back into the rain forest at the first sound of a boat engine."

They angled back toward the river and were soon struggling through the undergrowth, with the water's surface, sheened in starlight, not far to their left. John could see Eva's point about navigating, but walking close to the river didn't improve the terrain. Their feet sank in the mud, and more than once they tripped over trailing roots. They blundered into huge leaves that showered them with the rainwater they contained. They had no choice but to walk in their soaking-wet clothes and mud-caked shoes even when the ground was more level. The sounds of the night were almost deafeningly loud: the distant booming of howler monkeys, the resounding cry of bellbirds, and the distant eerie screech of a piha.

Salome stumbled into another unseen ditch, catching herself with her hands, but she yelped. "Ow! Thorns."

"Sh," said John. He promptly found his leg caught by a trailing vine and staggered sideways with a gasp.

"You two," Eva growled. "There's no need for—"

Her shriek was louder than the monkeys, cicadas, and birds put together; John almost jumped out of his mud-caked shoes.

"*Get it off me! Get it off!*"

<72>

John spun around, almost falling again, and focused his phone flashlight on Eva. What looked like a black splatter covered the top of her blonde head, and for a moment he thought it was river mud—until it *scuttled*.

Salome squealed and darted forward to swipe at the spider with her shaking hands. It dropped from Eva's head to her shoulder, then seemed to vanish. He had never seen anything move so fast. He shuddered, peering down at the ground, though the darkness was so encompassing that he'd never have a hope of finding the spider.

"Ewww," moaned Salome. Eva was still trembling, raking her hands through her hair.

"Hush," said John suddenly. He went still, and eventually even Eva calmed down enough to listen.

He didn't know why he bothered to call for quiet so often; the forest sounds were so loud and so constant it was unlikely anyone would hear their clumsy footfalls or their shaky breathing. But that scream of Eva's had rivaled the howler monkeys . . .

In response to a nearby rustle of branches, John spun around unsteadily, his heart pounding.

"Who's there?" he called.

A torch beam glared suddenly in his face. *Baeker and Field!* he thought with a surge of panic, swinging his own flashlight around.

But the man who stepped out of the undergrowth was neither agent. Instead of a sharply cut suit and leather shoes, he wore a Barcelona soccer shirt, cargo shorts, and Havaianas flip-flops. He barked something at John, and John turned anxiously to Salome.

<73>

"What's he saying?" John knew Salome could always translate with IIDA's help.

Salome stared at the man, biting her lip as he spoke again, more calmly this time.

"I have no idea." She shrugged. "Even Mother can't help me. That's not Portuguese."

The man frowned and asked what sounded like another question. Salome shut her eyes, finally risking a brief communication with their "mother" IIDA, John guessed. The supercomputer would eventually decode the language, he knew, but it would take time.

The man's gestures, though, were perfectly understandable. He raised a hand and beckoned them sharply.

The three glanced at one another.

"Should we go with him?" asked Eva.

"He doesn't seem hostile," said Salome, "but even if he *is*, I don't see what alternative we have."

The man beckoned with his arms again, more urgently.

"I think he's from a local tribe," said Eva suddenly. "That would explain the language. Doesn't your programming recognize it at all, Salome?"

Salome shook her head. "No, but IIDA will get there. I just hope Mikael isn't alerted to the IIDA activity."

"He's probably too preoccupied," said John. "And he can't possibly monitor *everything* IIDA does. He'd have to be a super-computer himself."

"That's what I'm hoping," said Salome, biting her lip.

"Even if he notices," shrugged John, "a quick translation won't give him our location—using GPS sure would."

<74>

"True. In the meantime, I think we should go with this guy. I *hate* this forest."

"I guess he might be able to help us," suggested John. Uncertain, he nodded at the man and moved a couple of steps closer. The man smiled. Now John could see the flecks of red paint on his cheekbones: arrow shapes drawn casually but deftly.

"Those definitely look tribal," he remarked to Eva, and she nodded.

"All right," she said. "I'm making the decision for all of us. Let's go with him."

The hut he led them to was hard to make out in the darkness, but when John shone his flashlight over the walls, he could see it was built of bamboo, pale and sturdy in a cleared patch of forest. He swallowed hard. At least it didn't look like the lair of a supervillain. Their unexpected host swung open the door and beckoned them inside.

John didn't know what he'd been expecting—mud floors, an open campfire?—but to his astonishment the hut's interior didn't look dissimilar from his mother's house. Smaller, for sure, but there was a floral-patterned armchair and a matching sofa, a small television, and scattered colorful rugs. A fridge hummed in the corner, next to a small gas stove. Beside the fridge sat a small cage on a wooden table. Salome gave a gasp of delight and crouched beside it; the straw shivered and rustled, and a brown and white guinea pig wriggled out, its nose twitching inquisitively.

"It's adorable," she gushed.

"He's naughty," said their host, "but cute."

<75>

The three stared at him in astonishment, but he only gazed back blankly. John nudged Eva.

"IIDA's been working," he murmured. "We got the translation download."

Salome turned her head and grinned at them. "I knew Mother could work fast."

"I was surprised to come across you in the forest, especially at night. Can I offer you something to drink?" asked the man. "I'm Tiago."

"I'm Salome, and this is Eva and John." Salome replied fluently in Tiago's language, as she nodded at her friends. "And I'd kill for a cool drink!"

Grinning, Tiago opened the fridge and brought them tumblers of juice, sharp and sweet. They sipped gratefully, trying not to peer too nosily around the hut.

"I'm embarrassed that I expected a mud hut," whispered John.

"Yeah, me too." Salome smiled at Tiago. "You have a lovely home."

He shrugged modestly. "It is comfortable. But what are you doing in the forest? Are you lost? If so, I can guide you to where you need to go."

John exchanged a hopeful glance with Salome and Eva. "We're not lost, really"—he indicated his phone—"but we could use some pointers to get us to here the fastest way." Turning on the screen, he enlarged the GPS map.

Tiago rose and came closer to peer at the screen. His eyes widened, and John thought his face grew paler.

"No." Tiago stood up sharply. "You must stay away from that place."

<76>

"What?" John gave a laugh. "It's just a school."

"A school? That is no school. To teach evil?"

Salome frowned. "No, you must have misunderstood. It's just a . . . a branch of our own school. A normal school. We are visiting; we're expected."

Tiago took a step backward. "That part of the jungle, it's bad. You must not go there."

John opened his mouth, then closed it again. He didn't want to make things worse by implying that Tiago believed in evil spirits . . .

"The place is evil," said Tiago, flatly. His eyes had grown hard. "Bad things live there. All of us who live in the forest, we know stories."

"But that's all they are," John insisted. "Just stories. I know these schools are secretive, but they're not evil."

"Believe the stories, don't believe the stories. It is your choice." Tiago moved toward the door; it was clear he wanted them to leave. "But I will not guide you there."

<77>

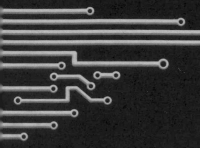

Eleven

"At least they made it to Brazil," sighed Akane, slumping down onto the edge of Slack's bed. "There's nothing Mikael can do about that."

Slack peered at her over the lid of his laptop. "I'm sure he'd like to try. Apparently, he's livid."

"Not half as livid as Tina." Akane grinned. "Dmitri was waiting outside Mikael's office, and he heard the whole Skype call between them. Voices were raised, apparently. A *lot*."

"But mostly Tina's, I imagine." Slack chuckled. "She would *not* be impressed that Mikael managed to mislay their son."

Akane tipped her head back to stare at the ceiling. The lighting in the Wolf's Den was the closest technology could get to natural sunlight, but she still missed the open air and real daylight. "The whole school's talking about their disappearance. And because we're not letting on where they are, you and I are the villains of the tale." She waggled her eyebrows at Slack and grinned.

"Because we covered for our friends? We're so *selfless*," cried Slack dramatically. "When we would have dearly liked to be on the adventure ourselves."

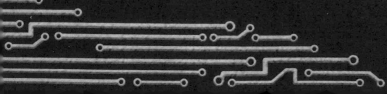

"Howard McAuliffe is scandalized," Akane told him. "But I was passing Ms. Reiffelt on the atrium ramp, and I swear she gave me a wink and a thumbs-up behind her folder."

"That's because we'd have been perfect East German spies. Back in the day she'd have recruited us." Slack giggled. "Does history relate how Mikael reacted when he got to his nonexistent Shanghai conference?"

"History does not relate," grinned Akane, "but Dmitri does. That was part of the conversation with Tina that he overheard. Apparently, Mikael was ranting like a maniac. He did *not* enjoy falling for one of John's pranks."

"I'm glad you're here to keep me up to date with the gossip," said Slack. "I'm so bored in here. Nobody else would tell me."

"It's nice hanging out with you," blurted Akane. She reddened slightly. "I mean, getting to know each other better. Without the others here. I—"

Her voice dried, but Slack, too, was blushing slightly. "I know exactly what you mean. And I'm, uh . . . I'm enjoying your company too, Akane."

She turned away quickly and cleared her throat. "So you haven't seen many others while you've been in here?"

"Oh, a few. Adam and Leo came by the other day to update me on Project Husky—oh, and also to laugh at my predicament, but never mind—but they wouldn't say much at all about John and the others vanishing. I thought they'd be jealous." Slack frowned. "But they didn't seem to mind one bit that John, Salome, and Eva are off having illicit fun somewhere unspecified. If anything they looked—well, *smug.*"

<79>

Akane raised her eyebrows. "That's odd. From everything you've told me about those two, I'd have expected them to be seething with jealousy. Don't they like to be the big fish and the center of everyone's attention?"

"Yup, and they were totally Lykos's teacher's pets. I don't like it when those two are happy about *anything*."

"You don't suppose they—" Akane stopped.

Slack's eyes had widened, and he twitched his hand slightly; Akane understood immediately that he wanted her to be quiet. His face stretched into an insincere smile as he stared over her shoulder.

"Adam," he said. "Leo. You're back. It's nice that you care so much about me."

There was huffing and laughter coming from behind Akane. She turned to see the two boys, instantly distinctive wearing their preppy designer polo shirts and sharply cut chinos. *Honestly,* she thought, *it's like they're the only forty-year-olds in the school.*

"Still waiting on news from the techs," said Adam with a sly look, "about the damage to the AI huskies. How are things with you, Slack?"

"Yeah," added Leo, "how's that broken butt of yours?"

"Fine," said Slack through gritted teeth. "Or it soon will be."

"Bet you're missing John and the girls." Adam's eyes glinted with what could have been curiosity or malice. "Are they having fun?"

"How would I know?" Slack shrugged. "I don't even know where they are."

Leo snorted. "Sure. Well, if they weren't *underage*, I guess they'd have a tropical drink for you."

<80>

The kick Adam gave Leo's ankle was brutal. Akane couldn't see it from where she sat, but Leo's face said it all. She took a quiet breath and narrowed her eyes. "What did you say?"

"Maybe *wherever they are* it doesn't have a cocktail bar," said Adam loudly through gritted teeth. "Well. I hope they're behaving. Be a bit embarrassing if John Laine himself had to be expelled."

The two of them looked puzzled. Akane turned to Slack, feeling her face grow pale.

"What the? Why would Adam and Leo mention caipirinhas? How could they suspect they're in Brazil?"

"I haven't told *anybody*," Slack insisted. "I haven't been out of the infirmary!"

Akane scowled. "That was no lucky shot in the dark from Leo. Something's going on." She pulled her MindReader from her pocket and fitted it behind her ear. "I'm going to try to contact Ana."

Ana responded remarkably quickly to the mental ping. A flurry of tropical emojis popped into Akane's head.

—Hey, friend! 🖤 🌺 🌺 🌺 🌺

—Hey, Ana! Did the others get there yet?

—No, but we can't wait! It's going to be so great to meet fellow students from the Wolf's Den. We want to hear more about it!

—Just a quick question. **Akane took a nervous breath.**
—Speaking of the Wolf's Den, has anyone else from here been in touch?

—Nobody! 🗯️ 🌑 Why? We're keeping your secret!

—You're sure you haven't had contact from . . . Irma Reiffelt, maybe? Or even a former teacher like Yasuo Yamamoto? Or . . . Roy Lykos?

<81>

—Hah! 😑 I hear Roy Lykos is doing time, as you say! No, no one has contacted us. But what about your friends Salome, Eva, and John? How is their journey? When will they get here?

Akane exchanged an anxious glance with Slack.

—I don't know, Ana. We haven't heard from them since they touched down in Manaus, but I know they're on their way as fast as possible. They're so excited to meet you!

—Good! 😺😺😺 There was a long pause. —But I hope they get here soon 🙁

—Huh? Is there a problem?

—No, no! Another hesitation. —Or maybe, just a little. It's just that Eva's parents are becoming suspicious. They are impatient, and they're not sure they trust that we are telling the truth.

—It's been such a long journey! protested Akane. —Reassure them Eva's on her way!

—Of course. I'm trying, I promise. But I'm only a student. This time, the silence stretched so long Akane was afraid Ana had signed off. —Akane, urge them to hurry. If they can't see their daughter very soon, Eva's parents are threatening to leave!

<82>

Twelve

"I wish we still had the boat," groaned John. "We could have stolen it from under Baeker's and Field's noses . . ."

"Don't be silly," Salome told him. "And stop complaining. It would have been much worse walking if Tiago hadn't arranged for us to borrow the kayak."

"Took a bit of persuading," John reminded her. "He really did *not* like any talk of the Ma'yaarr Complex, did he?"

"He was just superstitious," shrugged Eva. "He was talking nonsense."

"Of course he was," agreed Salome brightly, although a little tremor of anxiety rippled through her again. Tiago had been downright unnerving, the way he talked about the Center. And the river wasn't, to be honest, making her feel any better. The water was so still and opaque that it was far too easy to imagine monsters lurking in the depths. Every time she dipped her paddle, Salome expected it to come up with something's teeth attached to it. The forest canopy almost obliterated the sky over this smaller tributary, and the shadows made the air dark green and dank. The animal noise was constant, and the atmosphere was thick and moist. "How's your app looking, John? Are we getting close?"

"I really think we are." John peered at his phone screen. "The signal's amazing here, by the way. Another indication, I'm guessing. Maybe a mile more?"

"Yep. The closer we get to the Center, the stronger it'll get." Salome shrugged and stretched her aching shoulders. "It makes sense."

"This forest creeps me out," said Eva. "I hope we get to the Center soon."

"I know what you mean," said Salome. "It doesn't matter how noisy the birds and the cicadas are; it's too quiet! And the water . . . it's just so still."

It was as if she'd triggered a curse with careless words. Around the kayak the water suddenly exploded into churning foam, as if thousands of tiny creatures had sprung to life. Salome could feel the kayak shudder, and she dropped her paddle and clutched the gunwales.

"What the—"

"What *are* they?" yelled John. He half stood up, then abruptly sat back down.

The kayak was shuddering now, rocked by the thrashing of the mass of fish. Because they had to be fish, didn't they? *Not caimans!* thought Salome desperately. *Or anacondas . . . surely, they're too small for that? Surely!*

Eva gave a sharp scream as the kayak tilted. "Are they piranhas?"

"Dunno!" John had dropped his paddle too. He peered over the edge of the kayak. "Do piranhas have *really* red eyes?"

<84>

Salome gasped. John was right: the fish's eyes weren't just scarlet; they *glowed*. She was sure they were flinging themselves deliberately against the kayak. *They're trying to capsize us! What kind of fish does that?*

"We have to get out of the boat!" she cried.

"And go in the water?" shouted John. "No way!"

The kayak was shuddering violently now; John's knuckles were white from holding on.

"Yes, stay in the boat," cried Eva. "So long as we stay here, we'll be—"

The red glow of the fishes' eyes intensified, all at once. Tiny explosions lit up the murky water, and Salome gave a shout of fear as she saw hundreds of tiny wakes form.

"They're shooting at us!"

"That's not possible," gasped John. "Are those little *torpedoes?*"

That was exactly what they looked like, thought Salome as panic surged through her. But at least they were tiny . . .

They hit the kayak's sides with an impact that made it tip wildly, first one way and then the other. John screamed, trying to steady it with both hands. Salome felt water flood over her sneakers and soak her feet.

"They've punctured it. We're sinking!"

Water was gushing in through hundreds of tiny holes, too fast to bail out.

"Right," said Eva. "Decision made."

"No—!" began Salome.

But Eva had already hopped over the side of the kayak. With a splash she jolted onto the river bottom, and she swayed for a moment, waist-deep. Then, awkwardly, she began to run-wade toward the bank.

<85>

"Come on, John!" Salome followed her as the kayak wallowed around them. *Those things didn't eat Eva, they didn't eat Eva . . .* And sure enough, as she flailed panicking through the water, dragging her pack, the fish held back. As a shoal, they drew away, eye-lights still glowing fiercely through the green murk as if to light her way.

She scrambled to the bank and crawled out after Eva, dripping and gasping. Eva was shaking water from her hair, shivering more with fear than cold. Behind her, Salome heard John flop onto the bank, panting.

"Ugh, ugh! What *were* those things?" Salome half rose, swaying on her knees.

Silvery laughter pealed out, and she stared. All she could see was a pair of sturdy Timberland boots at the end of slender tanned legs. Salome raised her eyes slowly.

A woman stood there, laughing in delight. No, thought Salome—not a woman, but a girl of about their own age. She was strikingly pretty, her sleek mahogany-brown hair pulled back into a ponytail to show off her sharp slanted cheekbones. Her almond-shaped golden eyes sparkled with amusement.

"Hello, new friends. Welcome to the Ma'yaarr Complex!"

"That was not funny," spluttered Salome. Staggering to her feet, she swiped the weeds from her arms in disgust.

"Yes. You scared us!" Eva accused the girl.

Salome turned to John, but he was gazing at the girl as if someone had slapped him in the face with a large red-eyed fish. "I dunno," he said, a blush reddening his cheeks. "I guess I can see the funny side."

<86>

Salome rolled her eyes in exasperation, then glared at the girl—but she was still chuckling.

"It really is very good to meet you at last. You have taken your time getting here! I am Mirandinha, the principal of the Complex!"

"Principal?" Eva wrinkled her nose skeptically. "You look very young."

"Here at the Ma'yaarr Complex we choose our own leader," smiled the girl. "And the students have chosen me, because they're exceptionally smart!" She gave another burst of laughter. "And so are you, although I hear you don't recognize AI fish when you see them."

Salome noticed that John clenched his fist, as if to calm himself. *Not totally starstruck, then*, she thought grimly.

"We were taken by surprise," he said, "that's all. They're amazing. Much better than the AI huskies at the Wolf's Den, I admit." His face relaxed to a grin, and when Mirandinha rewarded him with one of her radiant smiles, he blushed again.

"We thought we'd give you a proper Ma'yaarr greeting," she laughed. "It helps us see what you are made of." She positively beamed at John, but the sidelong glance she shot at Salome and Eva was far more skeptical. Salome felt a tiny shiver of resentment.

"Now don't look so uneasy," said Mirandinha warmly, reaching out to clasp Salome's and Eva's hands. "Come along! I will show you your new home—the Ma'yaarr Treetop Complex!"

John headed enthusiastically after the girl, and Salome and Eva followed with rather more trepidation. A track had been cleared through the forest, the grass well trodden under their feet and the branches hacked back with machetes, but the canopy still interlocked over their heads. Salome found herself longing for a little more view of the sky.

<87>

When the trees at last opened up, they saw a tall brand-new wire fence. Beyond it the trees had been cleared far more efficiently, and huts, walkways, and streams were visible beyond the wire. Vines and flowers draped the fence, as if the rain forest were still trying to reclaim the semi-civilized sprawl. As Mirandinha called out and young students rushed to swing the barred gates open, Salome halted and sucked in a breath.

The graveled pathway broadened within the gates, flanked by two sentry huts. Along both sides of the track, students were lined, clapping and cheering as John, Eva, and Salome walked hesitantly into the complex. They trooped inside, staring in disbelief at the rows of grinning, welcoming faces. Mirandinha walked ahead of them, head high and arrogant, but Salome could not help the broad smile that spread across her face. It was impossible to resist the waves, the applause, and the broad grins of their new fellow students. The roar of their welcome surpassed even the constant racket of the jungle creatures.

"There will be no language problems," Mirandinha told them. "All students here are required to learn English rapidly, as the most universal digital language. I myself developed a special two-week digital speed-learning process, with a linguistics expert who . . . formerly worked here."

"Oh," Salome murmured to John, a little disappointed, "I won't be needing my special IIDA talent for translation!"

"Never mind," muttered John back; he couldn't repress his broad smile. "Even if you can't show off your superpower, I already like this place."

"It's not bad, is it?" agreed Eva, who had reddened with embarrassment. "Though I'm not sure I want this kind of attention to go on for too long."

<88>

"I'm sure it won't," said Salome with a chuckle. "They're just making us feel welcome. And it's . . . nice."

"So is the whole place," enthused John, staring up at the rope-and-wood walkways slung between the huts.

The complex smelled of freshly sawed timber and sunlight. Mirandinha led them across neat bridges spanning sparkling streams. The palm-thatched circular huts themselves were large and looked slickly appointed. Salome noticed a sophisticated electrical plant partly concealed by a glittering waterfall. Students around a natural rock-walled swimming pool sipped on fruit punches and gossiped around laptops, while their friends swam lazily in the green water; others played beach volleyball on a neatly maintained sandy court. Through the gleaming windows of the huts she caught glimpses of huge flat-screen TVs, woven mats, comfortable upholstered sofas, and the very same white relaxation pods she knew from the Wolf's Den.

"Food, candy, and sodas are unlimited," said Mirandinha, gesturing at the relaxing students, "and you are welcome to join any of the pool parties when you are not studying or helping maintain the Complex." Halting suddenly, she barked out an order at a younger bespectacled boy: "Piotr! You're supposed to be on roof maintenance." He nodded eagerly. "And when you see Alina, tell her the electrical connection to Huts 17 and 18 needs attention."

Piotr scampered off without complaint, and Mirandinha turned to the newcomers. "We maintain the whole place ourselves," she explained. "There's plenty of time for fun and games, but the work is hard. This is how I think it should be."

John nodded, but Salome frowned. "And when do you get time for lessons?"

<89>

"Study here is a twenty-four-hour business," said Mirandinha. "All lessons are mandatory, and failure to attend scheduled lectures incurs penalties. Given the student privileges here, I don't think that's unreasonable."

"So the teachers are strict?" asked Salome.

Mirandinha let out a bellow of amusement. "No teachers! I proposed to the governors that the students were smarter than the staff. I persuaded them, of course, because I am smarter than *they* are too! So now we run this place ourselves, *very* successfully."

"Oh my," was all Salome could say. She shot a glance at Eva, who raised her eyebrows.

"I'm never going back to Alaska," declared John. "My family can come visit me here. I'm requesting—no, *demanding*—a transfer."

"It does look pretty cool," agreed Salome warily. Now that the welcoming crowd had dispersed, she could see students hurrying to their assigned jobs and study. However, there was a nervous intentness in their faces that she found slightly disturbing.

"All mod cons," she remarked. "And lots of fun. When do you all get time to sleep?"

Mirandinha shrugged and laughed. "Who needs it?" she said airily. "Oh, don't look like that, Salome—of course students get all their *required* downtime."

"I'm not going to need any sleep," grinned John. "I mean, look at this place, Salome, Eva. I can't imagine wasting a single moment sleeping—my next project is gonna be remote recharging for humans!"

"I like it," smiled Mirandinha, gazing warmly into his eyes. "John, you and I are going to get along very well indeed."

<90>

Thirteen

"I am just thrilled that you are here," declared Mirandinha. "I have heard about you all, and this is serendipity."

She had thrown herself back into a hammock that was slung between two kapok trees by one of the pools. John, Salome, and Eva were perched a little more awkwardly on deck chairs. They faced Mirandinha and felt rather like job interviewees, thought Salome. "We're thrilled to be here too," she said guardedly, "but I'd especially love to meet Ana. She's the one who told us all about the Complex and invited us here."

Mirandinha waved a hand. "Ana's not here right now. She's busy. You'll meet her later."

Eva cleared her throat. "Not just Ana," she grunted. "We had a tip-off about a couple who were seen around here. They were searching in the rain forest for—for a girl."

"Oh, of course!" Mirandinha jumped gracefully down from the hammock. "I'm so pleased to see you I'd almost forgotten why! Ana did mention this to me, of course. And the couple you speak of are here, Eva!"

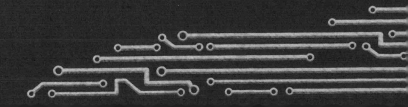

Eva sprang to her feet as if she couldn't help herself—but she looked nervous, chewing on her lip. "Mirandinha, can you take me to them? There is a possibility that . . . I may know these people. They may be . . ." Her voice trailed off as Mirandinha remained silent.

Salome glanced at her friend in concern, then frowned at Mirandinha. "What's wrong?"

"You believe they are your parents, do you not?" said Mirandinha nonchalantly. "Ana explained this to me."

Eva stared at her, with eagerness warring with resentment in her eyes. The Russian girl had never liked her emotions and hopes to be public knowledge, thought Salome sympathetically.

But, at last, Eva slowly nodded.

"I'd love to introduce you," said Mirandinha, sighing, "but alas, Eva, they left on a fishing trip just yesterday. Of course they will return, but—you see, they did not know you were coming. They had waited some time, but they could not bear the suspense any longer."

Eva's shoulders slumped, and for the first time since Salome had known her, she witnessed tears in her eyes. "But Ana said—"

"Ana can be impetuous," interrupted Mirandinha. "She makes promises she can't always keep. I'm so sorry, Eva—but when these people return from their expedition, I'll bring them straight to you. How about that?"

Eva was silent. She looked dumbstruck with disappointment. But John touched her arm gently.

"It's just a mistake, Eva," he murmured. "They didn't know we were coming, or I know they would have waited."

<92>

"They should have known," muttered Salome. "We were clear about why we were coming."

"Trust Mirandinha," insisted John, as he smiled at the brown-haired girl. "She'll bring you to your parents as soon as they come back, Eva; I know she will."

"Of course I will," shrugged Mirandinha. "And it'll only be a couple of days."

Salome narrowed her eyes in suspicion. It was true that John hadn't been party to the MindReader sessions with Ana, but he seemed very quick to dismiss Eva's concerns and believe Mirandinha.

But perhaps she herself was being oversuspicious. There was something about this girl's flip, casual certainty that irritated her—but wasn't Mirandinha a natural leader? Of course she was going to be like this. There were plenty of the same type at the Wolf's Den—certain of their abilities and not too concerned about other people's feelings. *Don't be silly*, Salome told herself. With everything going on here, details were bound to slip past a busy leader's notice. And it would be only a few days till the couple returned, if Mirandinha was, in fact, telling the truth.

Salome caught herself again. *Oh, don't be so cynical. Of course she's telling the truth.*

"There's plenty to keep you busy while you wait," said Mirandinha, a little more kindly.

"We're very happy to pitch in," enthused John. "With anything that needs doing. Roofing, electrics—you name it; we'll do it!

Speak for yourself, thought Salome a little sourly, but she, too, smiled at Mirandinha. "We're also here to learn, of course."

<93>

Mirandinha shot her a rather sharp look. "Yes, and that was just what I was about to say to John. Thank you, John, for your kind offer"—the look she gave John was far warmer—"but I think you're all most valuable working on our new coding project. Which very few others here actually know about, by the way, so keep this to yourselves."

"That sounds awesome." John's eyes lit up.

"What exactly *is* this project?" asked Eva, with a sidelong glance toward Salome.

"One you're going to love, because it's so deeply connected to all of you." Mirandinha's voice was filled with a tone of obsessive fervor. "We're developing complex programs to perfect a certain strand of genetic AI development."

John's eyes widened. "Genetic AI?"

"Yes." Mirandinha laughed. "The very AI-infused DNA you three have in your own bodies. It's common knowledge among certain higher echelons of the student body, you know!"

"Well, Dad hasn't kept it a secret since Morocco." John grinned.

Salome could feel cold ripples of uneasiness run down her spine. What John said was true, but why was Mirandinha so interested in improving it? "When you say 'perfect it,' you mean . . . ?"

"I—we, I mean—want to take this exciting technology to a new level," said Mirandinha. "And the best students at the Ma'yaarr Complex have been chosen to work on it."

"Chosen by you," pointed out Salome, gazing directly into the girl's golden eyes. "Because there aren't any teaching staff here."

"We are trusted to do the right thing." Mirandinha shrugged.

<94>

Trusted by whom? Salome wanted to ask; but given the hard light in Mirandinha's eyes, she figured she'd asked enough questions for now. *It's being run by students*—wasn't that what Sarah Lopez had said of the rogue Center? Salome was more and more suspicious that Ma'yaarr was the one, but she could hardly ask Mirandinha directly. She simply gave the girl a noncommittal smile and nodded.

"Let's go and look at the labs," suggested Mirandinha suddenly, linking her arm through John's and steering him away from the other two. "It's not just the DNA in you three that interests me, you know. John, you in particular can, I think, help me a lot with this project."

Watching John go willingly at the girl's side, Salome made a face at Eva, who nodded. Together they followed closely behind Mirandinha and John.

"Maybe she just likes him," murmured Eva.

"Mmm," said Salome darkly. "Maybe. But let's tag along anyway. I don't mind being a third wheel."

You may be a perfectly trustworthy person, Mirandinha, thought Salome as the girl gave her an irritated glance over her shoulder. *But we're not letting John out of our sight while he's in your clutches.*

<95>

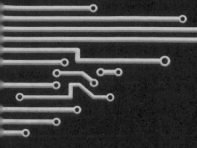

Fourteen

"It's nice to have some time to talk to you in private," Mirandinha told John with a dazzling smile. "Much as I like Salome and Eva, they seem terribly dependent on you."

"Hah!" John barked a laugh. "Those two aren't dependent on anyone—believe me!"

Looking puzzled, Mirandinha twisted a strand of hair between her fingers. "Well, they are very protective of you, then. They can't seem to leave us alone for thirty seconds."

The two of them had stretched out on a patch of grass beside the ornamental waterfall, taking a well-earned ten-minute break from their lab work. Salome and Eva had retreated to the sealed chamber where chemistry tests were performed. When Mirandinha had suggested a break, John had hastily agreed. The dark-haired girl fascinated him; maybe it was her intensity and her intelligence, or maybe it was just that shining brown hair and her beautiful, unusual eyes. He didn't care; it was just good to get a chance to talk to her after three days of being relentlessly stalked by his two steely eyed Ghost Network chaperones.

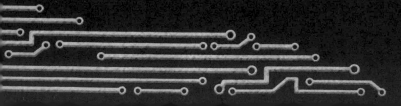

John stripped off his latex gloves and lay flat on his back, basking in the warm sunshine. Propping herself up on one elbow, Mirandinha gazed down at him. A huge blue butterfly flitted between them and landed on a nearby hibiscus blossom. John sighed with happiness.

"Don't worry about Salome and Eva," he told Mirandinha. "They're just protective of me; that's all. We've got past history in common, after all."

"And altered DNA," she retorted. "I guess you and they think that makes you some kind of siblings. When in fact it's just weird that you hang around with those immature girls."

John curled up abruptly to a sitting position, chasing away another butterfly. "That's not fair. They're my friends. We look after each other is all."

"That's not how it appears to me," she said, unperturbed by his glare. "To me—and I know teenagers well, since I run this place—it seems as if they're holding you back, John."

"You know teenagers because you *are* one," snapped John.

She shrugged. "I am a particularly intelligent teenager—like you, John. And you and I are head and shoulders above the rest of these admittedly bright students. Your brain far surpasses Salome's or Eva's, and you know this. Perhaps they don't *mean* to hold you back, but they do. Or perhaps—and it's just a possibility, you know—they are holding you back deliberately. Because they are jealous?"

"That's not fai—" John began to say again, when he realized he was repeating himself. And he didn't want Mirandinha to think he was the kind of boy who couldn't say something original. He turned his head away and said in a low voice, "It's not

<97>

like that. We've been through a lot together. Hey, there is a way to distract their attention from me, you know." He gazed at her again. "You could let Eva see her parents."

"If they even are her parents," sniffed Mirandinha dismissively. "And, besides, you know I can't. The floods downriver have prevented their return; I explained that to all of you. They will return to the Center when the waters go down a little. You wouldn't want them taking risks, would you? I'm quite sure *Eva* wouldn't like that."

He chewed on his lip. "But you'll take Eva to them as soon as they return, won't you?"

"Of course I will. Don't you believe me, John?" She scowled at him. "You did at first. Is it that Salome complains about me and says I'm untrustworthy? She doesn't like me, John. Come on, you're stronger and smarter than this. Like I said, smarter than *them*." She slowed her voice, emphasizing each syllable clearly. "Which. Is. Why. They. Are. Jealous. Look, John, do you even know what you're capable of? Because I can *show* you."

John rolled his eyes and laughed. "I still think that's crazy talk. But, go on, Mirandinha; show me." Mischievously, he glanced at his watch and added, "Otherwise, Salome and Eva are going to come in search of us, in five . . . four . . . three . . . two—"

Giggling, Mirandinha jumped to her feet and dragged him up. She led him with a run around a cluster of hexagonal wooden huts and over a small arched footbridge, then pounded across one of the suspended walkways toward a larger circular hut.

He followed her as she breezed through the swing door, letting it rattle behind her. A few kids glanced up from their desks, but when they caught sight of Mirandinha, they hurriedly

<98>

stared back at their laptop screens, tapping even more urgently at the keys.

Mirandinha nodded and folded her arms, seeming happy at her galvanizing effect. "Look at this, John. These students are all working on stuff that's light-years ahead of what the other Centers deal with. And you could be part of it!"

Tentatively, John approached one of the students; the ten-year-old's neck reddened, but she didn't turn around. Instead, she hammered even more rapidly at the keys. John felt his AI processing her physical responses. He sensed a code kick in somewhere in his head and start its own clinical analysis.

But he barely needed it. He was still human enough, John realized, to know that this girl was scared.

He leaned over her shoulder and watched her screen. "This is amazing," he enthused, more for the student's benefit than for Mirandinha's.

But it was Mirandinha who replied. "Yes, and I want you to help me with these programs, John. Think of what we could accomplish together!"

"I think I realize that," said John softly, "and it does seem really tempting . . ."

"Then stay with us!" Mirandinha strode around to stand in front of him; the younger student almost flinched, but Mirandinha ignored her. "Do you trust me, John?"

Do I?

John stared at her in silence for a long time. His inner AI that had interpreted the student's anxiety was now focused on the tall, confident girl who stood before him. Mirandinha's head was tilted slightly, almost as a mischievous challenge. She pouted

<99>

a little as he watched her, but he couldn't help it: for the time being, he was speechless.

His head felt so light, as if it were detached from his own body. The world around him became hazy, and the hum of computers and the click of keys became distant, irrelevant sounds. The coding within him rippled, finding connections, analyzing every one. Faster and faster it scrolled, seizing on links, downloading whatever IIDA software it needed.

And John could have sworn that the program *shuddered* with uneasiness. The artificial intelligence was echoed instantly by a chill that ran through his physical body.

It had taken only moments to get confirmation from both aspects of himself—human and computer—yet he said it anyway:

"Of course I trust you, Mirandinha."

Some things were just instinctive, after all; there were things neither his own brain nor IIDA could take into account. Like Mirandinha's smile and the way it warmed him right to his toes. Like the gentle touch of her hand on his arm as she gazed at him quizzically. Like the fact that she *trusted* him, that she *respected* him in a way that even his own father couldn't manage.

And, John thought with rueful amusement, the way her golden eyes shone and her hair gleamed. That grin was irresistible. She knew she'd won him over entirely, and she knew he knew it too.

John grinned right back, as they both turned away from the nervous student.

"Come on, then, Mirandinha. Where do I start?"

<100>

Fifteen

"I am tired of waiting," declared Eva, flopping back onto her bunk in the tree house she shared with Salome. "There's nothing online about these floods downstream. They can't be that serious! Why are my mother and father messing around like this?"

"Maybe they aren't," said Salome darkly. She sat up abruptly, dangling her legs over the edge of her own bunk. "Eva, I don't like the fact that your parents disappeared just as we arrived. Something's going on, and I don't like it. I don't even like this place—not nearly as much as I thought I would."

Eva rose and scuttled over to Salome's bed, sitting down beside her so that she could talk more quietly. "It's not the place. It's that girl Mirandinha."

"I know exactly what you mean," muttered Salome. "I can't stand her, and I don't trust her. Did you hear what she said to me yesterday, when I asked where she and John had been? She said, 'Nowhere you need to know about, little girl.' The nerve!"

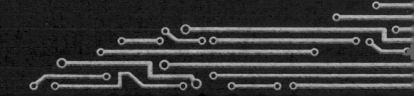

Eva was watching her intently. "I also noticed," she said softly, "that John said nothing. He looked embarrassed, but he looked away and pretended not to hear."

"Yeah." Salome shrugged and let her shoulders slump. "I don't know what's come over John."

"I do," said Eva. "Mirandinha, that's what. She is very pretty. And she has, uh . . . a very energetic personality."

"That's one way of describing it," grunted Salome.

"Much more so than the others," emphasized Eva with a scowl. She rubbed her temples. "They are friendly enough, yes, and they welcomed us. But with all their volleyball and pool parties, they don't seem very happy. I have watched many, many people pretend. And these students are playacting. Because they're afraid, Salome. They always keep an eye our for Mirandinha, and yet they shrink away when she approaches. They pretend to be content and at peace because they are simply scared."

Salome blinked at her. "I think you're right," she murmured. "There's another thing, Eva. What's happened to Ana? Is she with your parents? Why wasn't she here to welcome us? She sounded so enthusiastic about us coming, yet she hasn't shown her face!"

"There's only one thing to do," stated Eva, standing up and rubbing her hands together. "We will go and look for her ourselves. *Ana* might be more forthcoming about what's happening with my parents."

"All right," said Salome, rising to her feet. "But we must be careful, huh? I know we're supposed to be able to go anywhere in the Center, Eva—but I have a sneaking feeling Mirandinha won't like it."

"Oh, I'm sure of that." Eva snorted. "So come on."

Together they crept out of the tree house and slid down the steep ladder. The night was damp and warm, filled with scented passionflowers. The sound of crickets and tree frogs was almost deafening. At least the local wildlife would help give them some cover, Salome thought. Their light steps were not even audible above the racket of the chirping and piping.

"This way," murmured Salome, tugging Eva's sleeve to lead her over a narrow, arched bridge toward one of the waterfalls. The western side of the campus, with its thinner assortment of huts that looked less sophisticated than the rest, was one they hadn't yet explored. Mirandinha had shrugged dismissively when Salome asked about it, saying it held nothing more interesting than maintenance sheds. This, thought Salome, was as good a reason as any to investigate.

The tracks in this area were not as well lit as the rest, but they were easy enough to follow. Pale packed mud and sand gleamed in the starlight. The path was smooth and level between the profusion of foliage and grasses that lined it. On silent feet, Salome and Eva crept toward one of the distant square huts.

"Where are you going?"

The voice was clear and high, the voice of a child. Salome halted, peering into the shadows. He sounded even younger than the junior students did. As Salome peered down, she made out a small innocent face with huge eyes beneath a patterned bandana. The gun he was toting just had to be a toy. A computer prodigy, she wondered, or a local kid hired by Mirandinha to patrol the campus? He was half her height. She smiled indulgently.

"Olá," she said softly, so as not to spook him. "We're just looking around. We couldn't sleep. I guess you couldn't either, huh?"

<103>

The boy just stared at her.

Salome glanced at Eva, then back at the child. "We're looking for an older couple. A man and a woman . . . dark haired, both quite tall . . . uh . . ." Her voice trailed off into uncertainty. Then she shook herself. "Have you seen anyone like that here?"

The boy let out a sudden harsh bark of laughter that sounded odd coming from such a small child. "What if I have?"

Startled, Salome took a step back. The child didn't look quite so innocent as she'd first thought; his eyes flashed with an adult coldness. "We're just looking for them," she repeated. "There's no need to be rude!"

"Huh. You better hope you don't find them," he sneered. "Else you might end up like them."

"What?" Eva started forward, her fists clenched. "What are you saying?"

The boy turned. He simply stared at her, cocking his head slightly as if trying to make her out. A slow, unpleasant smile crept across his angelic face.

"You little—" Eva gasped and lunged toward him. "What have you done—"

Salome seized her arm and pulled her away. "He's just a little boy!" she hissed. "Eva, leave him. He hasn't done anything to them, and he can't possibly know anything—he's taunting us." She shot the boy an angry glare.

"Go away," he smiled. "Do what is best for you."

He stood right in their path, his arms folded. *He's only a little boy,* Salome told herself again. Yet somehow she did not want to try to walk past him . . .

<104>

"Come on, Eva," she muttered. "Let's go back. This can wait till morning." She stared at the boy again, her mouth twisting. "This isn't over, little one."

"Lil *Joao* is my name," the boy growled. "And yes. It is."

There was nothing Salome could say to respond to that— nothing she could say to a child, at least. Urging Eva away, she trudged angrily back toward their tree house.

But she could feel Lil Joao's sharp stare between her shoulder blades, long after his small shape was lost behind them in the darkness.

<105>

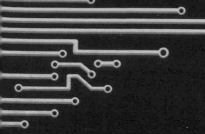

Sixteen

"I do not think this place is what it seems, Slack.
You must tell Akane."

"I don't like the sound of this, Eva. Shouldn't you three get out
of there?"

"Personally, I would love to. But I need to find out about my mother
and father. I can't leave here until I know what's happened to them!"

"This boy, this Lil Joao. You don't think he's hurt your parents?"

"He doesn't look big enough to hurt a squirrel, Slack. But . . . I
wonder. He frightens me. This whole place frightens me."

"Eva, you all need to get out of there. I really believe that."

"Even if I could, even if Salome agreed, I don't think we could
persuade John. He seems to be under some kind of spell. This girl . . .
Mirandinha—"

A ripple of laughter. "Oh, I know exactly what kind of spell that
idiot's under, from what you've told me. Listen, Eva—be careful, then.
Keep me and Akane up to date. We'll try to investigate from this end,
find out anything we can. But if it looks like things are getting really
dangerous, call us right away. Promise?"

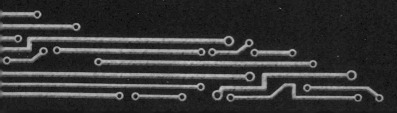

"*I promise to try, Slack.*"

"*Stay safe, Eva.*"

Mirandinha laughed silently to herself as she removed her MindReader and sat back in her leather chair. Around her, screens shimmered and glowed with text and images, but she didn't glance at any of them. Nothing was happening elsewhere on the campus; she could be sure of that. The only lingering minor irritation was those two girls and their suspicious minds.

But the MindReader devices had been pretty simple to hack. Salome and Eva didn't worry her, or not any more than any of the other students. They were easy enough to monitor via their own MindReaders. Whoever had developed that technology had made very few mistakes, but the barely detectable vulnerabilities had been glaringly obvious to Mirandinha. She always knew exactly where to look.

But, then, she had been taught by the best. If only she had the AI advantages of John and his friends . . .

. . . But that would soon be taken care of.

Lazily, she slid a hand across her console to pick up her cell phone. Its signature could not be traced; she had been taught, again, by the best.

Mirandinha punched the speed dial.

<107>

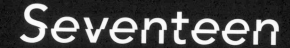

Seventeen

He just couldn't sleep, but it wasn't the hammock, thought John. The tight enclosing hold had been surprisingly easy to get used to, considering he'd never slept in one before. His body felt absolutely relaxed and secure and comfortable; it was his racing mind that wouldn't switch off.

Even Loki's antics couldn't distract him from thoughts of Mirandinha, he thought wryly. He let his favorite Norse mythology book drop to the wooden floor with a clunk. Rolling free of the hammock, he stood up, swaying a little. Yawning, he stretched his shoulders.

He'd known her for only a little over a week, yet his every waking moment seemed to be filled with thoughts of Mirandinha. Sometimes his sleeping ones too; she haunted his dreams.

I miss her when I'm not with her. John felt his AI crackle into life, a sort of alarm bell buried deep in his gut, but he shook himself in annoyance. He could ignore it. Of course he felt uneasy in a strange country, with people he'd never met before. That was all it was. In these past few days, in Mirandinha's physical presence,

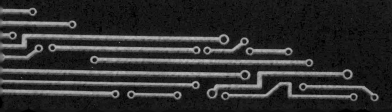

he always felt that anxiety subside. That was what he needed: to be with her.

He slid down the steep tree house ladder with his hands on the bars, not bothering to find the rungs with his feet. If there was one thing the ever-present AI did for him, it was to give him a sense of urgency. In fact, he'd learned that the easiest thing was to forcibly channel that alarm and the urgent prompts into an imperative to get himself into Mirandinha's company. If she didn't quite stifle his uneasiness, she at least masked it in a far more welcome manor.

Smiling to himself, he jogged along the walkway that led to her quarters.

The shuttered door opened easily and silently. He crept into the passageway that led to her workspace. If there was one thing he'd learned, it was that Mirandinha did not keep regular sleeping hours. In fact, he didn't understand when she slept at all; she always seemed to be working, thinking, or planning, and tonight was no exception.

He didn't usually hear voices, though. For a moment, as he listened to her murmured words, he hesitated. Was someone there in her control room with her? But only Mirandinha's voice was audible. He furrowed his brow and moved forward in the shadows.

"We're going to have to bring forward the plans, that's all. There's no point in complaining. You're the one who taught me the importance of flexibility and adaptability." She gave a rippling laugh; then there was a long moment of silence.

"If you'd left everything to me instead of sending those interfering men—oh *meu Deus*, they were a waste of space and time."

<109>

Silence again.

"Yes, big-time daddy issues, that one—and not a problem. It's the others who concern me. They're making trouble, talking outside of school. *Yes.* You heard me. That's why we need to advance the schedule."

John swallowed hard, though his throat felt hot and dry. This was an innocent conversation; it had to be.

"Lil Joao is a very helpful boy," snapped Mirandinha, "and he's *very* loyal, but even he can't be everywhere at once! And they aren't always together!"

No, thought John, with a rush of relief. He didn't know this boy Joao. Mirandinha wasn't talking about him, Salome, or Eva; she was discussing some other students. A few troublesome ones and one with "daddy issues" . . .

Process it, John. Process everything . . .

He gulped again, so hard he was afraid it was audible. And, sure enough, he saw Mirandinha's back stiffen, her cell phone move slightly away from her ear. The silence this time was not due to someone on the other end of the conversation.

Don't be ridiculous, IIDA. She's a kid like me. And I get along great with her. In fact, I really like her—so butt out! You're making me paranoid!

Mirandinha turned her chair slightly. Shaking himself, John straightened his shoulders and walked confidently out of the shadows.

"Hi, Mirandinha. Couldn't sleep again!"

She eyed him for a moment, her thumb quietly pressing the disconnect button on her phone. She didn't smile.

"John. How long have you been there?"

<110>

He shrugged. "Just got here. What are you working on?"

"I had to . . . make a call." Her eyes narrowed as she stood up.

John. Think! And process!

Shut up, IIDA. I'm busy. "Oh?" he said aloud to Mirandinha. "About the project to enhance the AI?"

"No. Not that." She hesitated. "Not *our* project. Another one." Her eyes flashed with sudden anger. "Why are you creeping around in the middle of the night?"

"Told you—I can't sleep." John felt wounded. "Sorry. I didn't mean to disturb you. I—"

"What did you hear?" she demanded.

"Nothing. Well, I heard the word 'schedule.'" He laughed. "That didn't give much away. What is it, the Chinese project?"

She stared at him hard, for what seemed like a very long time.

"Yes," she said and smiled at last. "That one. Sorry, John, you caught me by surprise. I didn't mean to snap at you."

He grinned broadly. "No worries. You need any help?"

"I guess I could." Laughing, she indicated the screens. "The Chinese thing . . . I've hit a coding hiccup. I mean, I could sort it out, but it's late, and I'm kind of tired. I bet you could do it in your nonexistent sleep. Want to work it out for me?"

"Sure." He strode over to the monitor and peered at it. "Oh, I see the squiggly line already. Want to check, or shall I just go ahead?"

"You just go ahead, my knight in shining flip-flops." She laughed as she came to stand behind him.

He could sense her there, leaning on his chair back; he could even feel her light breath on the back of his neck.

<111>

She was talking to a sponsor, trying to sound superconfident and like a leader. That's all. IIDA's being overprotective.

He wasn't stupid. Of course he would be careful. Of course he would store those fragments of her phone conversation with the files in his head. *Just in case . . .*

But the truth was he neither saw nor wanted to see anything wrong. *She brought me in; it's my project too.*

And IIDA and her maternal fussing aside, my actual coding would alert me straight away if the project was bad . . .

I'm sure it would.

<112>

Eighteen

"It's really nice of you to invite us for dinner," John told Mirandinha a few nights later. His voice sounded very loud in the long silence that hung over the bamboo table. "The, uh . . . the avocados are great."

He turned his smile toward Salome, who stared at him. What was wrong with John these days? He seemed completely smitten with Mirandinha and wouldn't hear a questionable word said against her. It was crazy. Why on earth didn't John show any signs of having his own suspicions? It seemed improbable that he'd lost *all* his sound judgment, but Mirandinha's attitude wasn't something he seemed willing or able to discuss. Of course, John hadn't been menaced by that psycho shrimp Lil Joao in the middle of the night, but still . . .

The air-conditioning had been turned off—"Let's keep it natural," Mirandinha had said—and the slowly turning ceiling fans did little to dispel the heavy humidity of the evening. Mirandinha herself sat like a duchess at the head of the table, picking at platters of food that were brought by younger students. She seemed

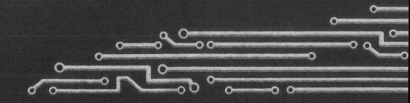

completely oblivious to the awkward atmosphere among the other three at the table.

"It's certainly a beautiful evening," ventured Salome, if only to say something. "Very *warm*."

"I love the heat," said Mirandinha. "It's one of the things I love about the Ma'yaarr Complex. I imagine it's much different from the Wolf's Den." She shuddered dramatically. "Isn't it terribly cold up there?"

"It's very fresh," said Salome. "The heat can be oppressive, don't you think?"

"Ugh! Not half as oppressive as all those teachers, though," said Mirandinha scornfully. "I hear Howard McAuliffe is the dullest speaker on the planet."

John just laughed.

"And the students are probably a lot smarter than the so-called adults," sniffed Mirandinha. "Just like here. Your students should do what we did and let the teachers go!"

"It still seems odd to me that the board of governors raised no objections to that," said Salome hesitantly.

"Oh, they did," laughed the girl, propping a foot up onto her bench. She popped a forkful of *patarashca* into her mouth. "But it's not like they had much of a choice. I pretty much gave them an ultimatum. Give us control or we simply leave and set up our own Center."

"Give *you* control, you mean," muttered Eva. She hadn't touched a mouthful of the food, Salome noticed.

Mirandinha gave the Russian girl a level, assessing stare. "Since I am their leader, yes. Effectively so. But I run this Center for the benefit of all its students, Eva."

<114>

"Really?" Eva's eyes sparked. "When you have tiny psychopaths watching their every move?"

"What on earth do you mean?" Mirandinha's eyes widened.

"That boy with the gun!" snapped Eva. "He shouldn't even be playing with a toy pistol, let alone waving that thing around!"

"Ah, Lil Joao?" Mirandinha giggled. John must have found her mirth infectious, because he laughed too. "Lil Joao is such a helpful boy. He likes to look after things for me. You mustn't mind him."

"He's a brat with too much power," gritted Eva through her teeth. "I have seen him ordering the older students around as if he's their colonel in chief."

"Everyone likes to indulge him," smiled Mirandinha, though there was a hard light in her eyes. "He's a very popular little boy."

"Oh, the kid who runs all the errands? He's all right," agreed John. "If you don't take him too seriously, Eva. He likes to feel important, that's all. Don't mind him; he's just a kid!"

Eva challenged him. "Am I the only one who remembers why we're here?" she snapped. "We came to find my parents—and one minute they're off on a fishing trip, the next they're delayed by floods, the next they are quarantined with the flu! I don't believe any of it!"

John looked anxiously at Mirandinha; she placed her hand lightly over his.

"You mustn't worry about your mother and father," she told Eva softly. "As soon as it's possible, you will be reunited with them. You would *not* wish to catch a tropical virus, and neither would the rest of us. You must think of the good of all, Eva."

<115>

"John," said Eva, ignoring the girl. "Why are *you* being so pathetic?"

He glared at her, but once again it was Mirandinha who replied. "Oh, Eva, John is a grown-up, and you should act like one too. What do you need parents for, anyway? Mine were useless. Completely absent when I was growing up, but it didn't matter because I didn't need them. I learned to be self-sufficient, as any human being should."

"I'm sure you had nannies and caretakers?" said Salome, horrified. "My parents had to work a lot too, but they always made sure I was looked after."

"Many nannies, many caretakers." Mirandinha shrugged. "I was always smarter than any of them. I always managed to give them the slip, and I chose my own food, my own bedtime, my own activities. If they didn't like it, they left." She smirked. "A lot of them left."

"Mirandinha has a point, Eva." John spoke up at last. "Look where my parents got me."

"John!" exclaimed Salome.

"You spoiled little boy!" cried Eva. "Your parents are the finest people you could possibly ask for, John Laine."

"My father abandoned us—"

"Because he had to!" Eva slammed her fist onto the bamboo table, making the platters of fruit scatter. "You are a horrible ingrate, John. Your father gave you everything, including your *life*—twice! He saved you! And your mother was always there to look after you."

John had the grace to look a little shamefaced, though he still glanced toward Mirandinha for approval. That only seemed to enrage Eva even more.

<116>

"You have *no idea* what it's like to have no family!" she exclaimed. "None of you do! So your father went missing for a while, John—so what? I've never known who my parents even are or why they left me. *Was* I abandoned, or was I stolen from them? I don't even know that much!"

John was opening and closing his mouth like a stunned fish. Salome felt bad for Eva, but she also felt a little ripple of satisfaction—John had thoroughly deserved that tongue-lashing.

Mirandinha had fallen silent, but within a few moments she got to her feet, resting her fists on the table.

"I think it's best if you all leave now," she said, staring down at her plate.

"I think so," said John. "It's been nice, Mirandinha, but Eva and Salome—maybe we're all tired."

"No," said Mirandinha coldly. "You too, John. I would like to be alone."

He looked startled, and hurt, but he got to his feet right away, as if he couldn't bear not to obey her. Salome frowned as she clasped Eva's hand and squeezed it, comfortingly. The girl was still trembling with fury.

"All right," said John dutifully. "I'm sorry about all this, Mirandinha. Thank you for a lovely meal."

Salome felt Eva's fingers tighten on hers so fiercely they hurt.

Yup—best we go now, she thought. *Eva's likely to tear John's eyes out if he says another word.*

<117>

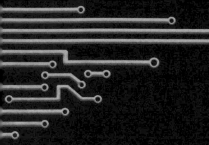

Nineteen

"Slack. Is your MindReader working?" Akane pushed
her chair back from her desk and turned to Slack, her brow
creased with anxiety.

Slack tossed aside his comic book and picked up his device,
slotting it behind his ear. "It's been fine. Hang on."

It seemed very still and calm in the study room they were
using to work in. Outside, around Little Diomede, an autumn
storm was raging, bringing the first real snow of the season.
However, not even a whisper of that howling wind reached them
in the depths of the Center. Even though they were surrounded
by state-of-the-art communications technology, thought Akane, it
was so easy here to feel cut off from the real world.

—It's working fine. Can you hear me?

Akane frowned in bewilderment. —Yes. So there's nothing
wrong with mine either. She hesitated. —Can you try contacting
John and the others again?

Slack went quiet. Akane watched his face progress from mildly
bored confidence, to confusion, to sudden wide-eyed alarm.

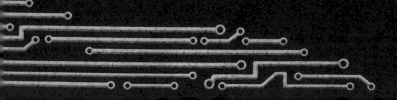

—No, I . . . In irritation, he tugged off his MindReader and spoke to her properly. "No, I can't get through at all. Is it a distance thing?"

She shrugged helplessly. "It was working just fine until now. Slack, I don't like this. It feels like contact has been cut off suddenly. Deliberately perhaps?"

"We're the Ghost Network, Akane," growled Slack. "I think we have to assume that anything that happens is deliberate."

"Why would John, Salome, and Eva break the connection? They wouldn't. We were supposed to be their contacts."

"There's something that's been niggling at me," Slack confessed. "Sarah never did know which Center was the rogue one. It's entirely possible it's this Ma'yaarr place, isn't it?"

"Salome did mention something vague about a rogue Center before she left for Brazil. The students were even running it," said Akane. "I admit that's been worrying me too."

"And if it *is* the rogue Center," murmured Slack, "just how rogue is it? Innocent anarchy under the control of brilliant students or . . . something more sinister?"

Akane grabbed her cell phone. "I wonder whether Sarah's dug up any more information since we spoke . . ."

Slack, who was nearly recovered from his fracture and already becoming bored and antsy, looked almost delighted at a hint of trouble. He stood up rather stiffly and came to stand over Akane's chair as she punched Sarah's name on the screen. Akane was slightly annoyed at his sudden lift in spirits, yet she found that she didn't resent his closeness at all. She leaned back a little, letting her shoulder come into contact with his arm. Was that a shiver she felt?

<119>

"Sarah, hi!" she said as the journalist answered, and as she put Slack's closeness out of her mind. She pressed the speaker button to let Slack hear.

"Akane? What can I do for you guys?"

"It's just . . . it might be nothing."

"It's never nothing with the Centers." Sarah laughed.

"Well, quite." Akane felt her heart beating hard, and it wasn't entirely because Slack was standing right behind her. "So I wondered whether you'd be willing to tell me something?"

"Go on . . ."

"The rogue Center." Akane shut her eyes and crossed her fingers. The words came out in a rush. "Would you tell me who gave you that inside information?"

Sarah's indrawn breath was audible. After that, there was only silence.

"I'm sorry, Sarah. I wouldn't ask, only we can't contact the others. John, Salome, and Eva are out there, and we don't know what's happening. And I swear, Slack and I won't tell another soul."

"Akane," sighed Sarah at last. "You know I can't reveal my sources."

"Not to the government or a court or anything," pleaded Akane, "but it's just us. We're really worried about the others. You know they went to the Ma'yaarr Complex in Brazil?"

"Without His Lordship Mikael's permission." Sarah laughed. "Yeah, I heard they'd sneaked off somewhere, but I didn't know they'd gone on an Amazon adventure. I hope they're OK."

"Well, some of the things they've said . . . have made Slack and I think Ma'yaarr's gone rogue. And there's been radio silence for a few days now. I'm not sure whether John, Salome, and

<120>

Eva are in any sort of trouble—we haven't heard anything like that—but it's unlike them to break contact for so long. And they were concerned about several things down there. Salome felt quite—threatened. And, well, I'm worried too. That they're in actual danger."

There was an indrawn breath at the other end of the line. "Again," said Sarah softly.

"Yes." Akane bit her lip hard. Now that she'd said it out loud—that her friends might be in real danger—she truly realized for the first time how serious it was. *Please please please . . .*

The silence lasted for several seconds again before Sarah cleared her throat. "All right, Akane. Since it's you guys, I'll tell you my source. It was a government official in the Department of Homeland Cybersecurity. Evan J. Whiteford."

Akane filed the name carefully in her head. "Whiteford?" She spelled it out.

"That's right. But you didn't hear it from me, 'kay?"

"OK, Sarah." Akane ended the call and sat staring at her blank screen. "That information was what finally drew Eva and the others down to the Amazon. Something bad's happening, Slack."

"Are we going to tell Mikael? He hasn't stopped fuming since he came back from Shanghai."

"I think we have to." Akane raised her eyes dolefully to Slack's. "I don't think we have a choice now."

"What in the heck are they doing in Brazil?"

Akane was beginning to realize that the Shanghai trick was nothing compared to what it had been designed to cover up. She thought she'd seen Mikael angry before, but he was really

<121>

taking it to the next level now. He paced back and forth behind his desk, with his jaw clenched, two red spots forming on his cheekbones.

"We told you," shrugged Slack. "It was the only way Eva could check out this story about her parents."

"How about just asking *me?*"

"You wouldn't have known, though, would you? And you wouldn't have let them go alone."

"You're certainly correct I wouldn't!"

"Eva had to know," Akane interrupted quietly.

"Why? Haven't I looked after her?" Mikael slumped into his desk chair and raked his fingers through his hair. "*Evan J. White-ford.* Whiteford . . ."

"Who is he?" asked Slack and Akane simultaneously. They exchanged a glance, half smiling despite the seriousness of the situation.

"I know the name. I just can't quite pin it down . . . I know I will. I'll remember at 3 a.m.—you know how that goes. But I'll tell you one thing." Mikael sucked in a breath. "The name gives me a bad feeling."

"He works for the DHCS, doesn't he?" Slack shrugged. "No reason for Sarah to distrust him."

"Be that as it may, I can't leave them down there. Looks like I have to turn around and get back on a plane again."

Akane tried to feel sorry for him but failed. *If you'd been more sympathetic to Eva in the first place . . .*

Mikael abruptly stood up again and clenched his fists. "Thank you for telling me—*eventually.* You two can go back to class. Me, I have a flight to catch."

<122>

Mikael pulled out a file, dumped the contents on his desk, and began to search for his passport. He'd thrown it in there during a fit of rage upon his return from Shanghai, and who could blame him? He should have known John better, should have had his suspicions aroused as soon as the kid started trying to be helpful with that completely unnecessary "keynote address" . . . Mikael growled to himself as he flung papers aside.

Here it was. He snatched the passport from his travel file in angry triumph. He must have been furious when he returned from Shanghai if he'd stuffed it carelessly into this sentimental old envelope of souvenir used tickets and old pictures. Maybe he'd still been mad at the whole system too: why the governments of the world couldn't dispense with ridiculous paper passports and simply install chips in their citizens, Mikael had no idea. He rolled his eyes—and caught sight of the photograph. It had half slipped out with the other old snapshots, where it must have been stashed for what—fifteen years? Mikael picked it up.

Evan J. Whiteford. Of course the name was familiar! So was the bristle-cut blond hair, and so were the cold, astonishingly blue eyes and the powerful broad shoulders. In the photo, the hand that gripped Roy Lykos's shoulder looked huge, even against Lykos's tall frame. And they were both grinning at the camera. They looked a little surprised at being caught side by side at a Washington cocktail party, but they'd brazened it out, laughing. Mikael remembered it all, now.

He remembered yelling Roy's name in slightly drunk surprise, remembered the guilty and conspiratorial light in their eyes as they'd turned toward his greeting. He recalled their swift and jovial banter about just having met. "Ha! Yeah, conflict of interest, eh? Don't tell the senator or his committee, Mikael, but Whiteford and I have discovered a shared passion for a good Manhattan!"

And he had another sudden, vivid memory—a far more recent one. Lykos's sly wink as the FBI agents clicked the handcuffs on.

"Oh, Mikael, my old friend. There isn't a prison in the world that can hold code."

<124>

Twenty

The cloying humidity had never gotten to Salome like this before, nor the deafening racket of the cicadas and frogs. The noise cut right through her aching head. It wasn't surprising; she hadn't slept since she'd clambered utterly exhausted into her hammock two hours ago. Every muscle in her head and neck felt tense with fear. But she had tried, again and again, and she couldn't keep her failure to herself anymore. She rolled back out of her hammock and snuck as quickly and quietly as she could to John's sleeping quarters.

"John. John," Salome whispered urgently in the darkness.

The lumpy shape of his hammock stirred slowly. "Wha—?" he mumbled.

"John," she said more loudly and urgently. "I can't reach Akane on the MindReader. It's blocked somehow."

"So the signal's wonky." He yawned. "Or she's busy or something."

"She's never too busy," gritted Salome, trying to hold on to her patience. "And I haven't heard from her in days, now that I think

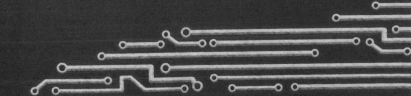

about it. And, also, the signal always works. It's linked through IIDA, not the mobile phone network."

Reluctantly, John untangled himself from his hammock and stumbled unsteadily to the ground.

"I'm sure everything's OK," he said, rubbing his eyes.

"You always are, since we got here." Salome glared at his shape in the shadow of the tree house. "I don't like it, John. Something's wrong."

He was rubbing his head now, as if he was trying to take in her words and not quite comprehending them. "Fine. Fine. I'll get ahold of Akane, and then we can both go back to sleep."

He rummaged in his bamboo chest for it. The MindReader, Salome realized, was at the bottom of the drawer, under his clothes. He hadn't bothered to use it. *His own invention . . .*

With a sulky look, John fitted the device behind his ear and focused. Even in the darkness, Salome saw the change that came over his face. Lazy disinterest turned to deep concentration and frustration, then to a nervous uncertainty.

"Mine's blocked too," he murmured. "It *should* work."

"Yes. It *should*." Salome glared at him. "Don't you get it yet?"

"We can make sure, then. I'm sure nothing's wrong. Mirandinha will fix it."

"Mirandinha probably *broke it!*"

"No, no. Let's go find Eva. We can fix this, Salome; I know we can—"

The door banged open behind them, causing them to shudder.

"*You two.*" A high commanding voice made them both spin around in shock.

<126>

Salome stared. Lil Joao held a heavy gun in both hands; despite its size, his fingers didn't tremble. Beside him stood a small dark-haired girl, also armed, with eyes even colder than his.

Lil Joao Number 2, thought Salome with a chill of fear. "What do you want?"

"You have to come with us." Lil Joao motioned his head toward the door.

"I don't think so," growled John. "What d'you think you're doing?"

"You think I won't shoot?" The small boy swung the gun barrel so it was aimed directly between John's eyes. Then he lowered it to point at his belly. "I don't have to kill you. You'll still be usable."

Usable? "He means it," said Salome quickly. "John, let's go. We can sort this out." She had no idea whether that was true, but staying put only to be shot by this tiny psychopath was not an option.

It was weird, she thought as the two children marched them out of John's room into the warm darkness of the Amazon night. John looked irritated, but he still didn't seem to be taking their situation very seriously.

"Quiet," commanded Lil Joao. He slammed open the door of Eva's sleeping quarters. "You," he barked. "You are to come with us."

Eva might have only just woken up, but her anger at the previous night's dinner had clearly not left her. She stood dazed for all of two seconds before giving a screech of fury.

"What are you—how dare you! You little brute! What did you do with my parents? You'll tell me—I swear you will!" Ignoring the

<127>

boy's gun, she flung a pillow at him. Salome was amazed the pistol didn't go off by accident. "Get out! Get out!"

For the first time, Lil Joao looked as if he had no idea what to do. He glanced at his small comrade, who seemed as bewildered as he did; then he raised his gun and fired it in the air.

The noise was explosive and deafening in the enclosed space; Salome's head rang as she clasped her hands over her ears. Tiny scraps of thatch and bamboo drifted down from the bullet hole in the roof. John looked too shocked to speak.

But Eva still didn't have that problem. "*You're threatening me, you otrodye, you—you brat!*"

Salome's heart pounded with terror. "Eva, do as he says!"

Eva's eyes turned to her, and she frowned in confusion. For the first time, the seriousness of the situation seemed to dawn on her. Lil Joao and his comrade had stepped into her room, with both guns pointed at her. Eva sucked in a breath.

"Come *now!*" demanded Lil Joao. He let another shot go into the air, and the whole room trembled with its roar.

"All right. *All right!*" Eva raised her hands.

She's going to obey, thought Salome with an overwhelming rush of relief that made her dizzy. Lil Joao was growling with anger as he jerked his gun to gesture toward the door.

But he was still completely focused on Eva, Salome realized. And he and his dead-eyed friend were right inside Eva's room, while Salome still stood on the walkway . . .

It's my only chance. Our only chance!

She made a split-second decision. Spinning on her heel, she raced barefoot down the walkway. It took Lil Joao a couple of seconds to realize what she was doing, but then his high-pitched

<128>

squeals of rage split the air. Salome grabbed hold of the rope barrier and somersaulted down to the grass ten feet below.

She landed with a grunt, rolling, but the ground was soft. Leaping to her feet, she bolted between two huts and ran for her life.

Gunshots rang out behind her, not nearly as loud in the open air, and she saw puffs of dust rise from the earth two or three feet to her left. *It's all right*, she thought desperately, *they're shooting at me, not at John and Eva. They'll be OK.* She raced faster than she ever had in her life, zigzagging as much as she dared, then dived for the shadows of the enclosing forest.

There was still the barbed wire fence to deal with, but at least those creepy children had stopped firing. It struck Salome that despite the yells and squeals and the actual *gunshots*, no students had come out of their huts to see what was going on. Were they used to it, she wondered? Or just afraid to look?

The latter, she guessed. Pausing to take a breath beneath the lush foliage while peering fearfully back at the lit walkways, she heard Lil Joao's high imperious voice, raised to top volume for her benefit.

"She cannot get out of the compound. We will round her up later, Lil Fernanda. *She won't escape—she can be sure of that.*

"And then Mirandinha will *deal with her.*"

<129>

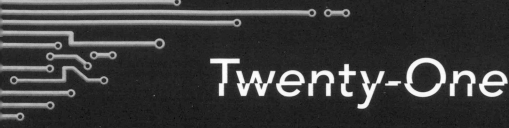

Twenty-One

I'll show you, you pint-sized maniac. Salome clenched her jaws as she clutched the sharp wire of the fence between her fingers. *I will get out of this compound, and Mirandinha will* not *get the chance to "deal with me"!*

Closing her eyes, she focused on her programming. *Come on, IIDA. Help me.*

She felt a sudden cool calmness trickle through her veins, and her mind was clear and sharp again. There was nothing to learn; there was only courage to be found. Gripping the wire, she hoisted herself up.

The thin wire cut into her flesh; before she'd climbed a few feet, she could feel warm blood between her fingers. Gritting her teeth, Salome kept climbing, hand over hand, digging her bare toes into the gaps in the wire. *This won't kill me. Lil Joao certainly will.*

She felt very far above the ground now; it was a mistake to look down, but she did. Her head swam, and she clutched the wire for her dear life. *Don't fall.*

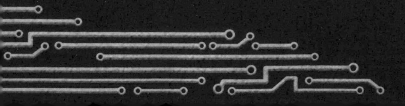

Prompts flickered in her mind's eye, and she took a deep breath. *Calm. Calm.* Her heart slowed, and she began to climb again, keeping her eyes fixed on the rain forest and freedom beyond the fence. It was only when her hand found the barbs of the top strands, and fiery pain dug into her palm, that she realized she was at the top.

There was nothing else. Eyeing the horizontal wires, she placed her hands carefully where there were no barbs. Then, taking another deep breath, she placed her feet against the fence, bent her knees, shoved herself back, and vaulted forward.

Spiked barbs tore at her waist and thighs, but she stifled the scream in her throat. IIDA's programming wouldn't let her flinch or fall. Her braids got tangled in one of the barbs, but she was over. Her feet dangled wildly on the other side of the fence, and her hands desperately tried to maintain her grip despite the tearing pain. Reaching up one shaking hand, she was able to tug her hair free. Her hands felt like they were on fire with pain, but she clambered doggedly down the other side of the fence. With three or four feet to go, the programming abruptly failed, drowned by the onslaught of panic and pain. She fell, landing with a thud on the damp mud and grass beyond the fence.

Salome lay there for a few minutes, breathing hard, trying to get control of herself. But she knew she had to move soon; Lil Joao would already be searching the campus, and he would not be pleased to realize she had breached the perimeter after all. Clambering awkwardly to her bloody feet, she stumbled into the forest.

It felt darker and more terrifying than it ever had, now that she was alone. The booming cries of disturbed howler monkeys

<131>

filled her ears as she ran, tripping and stumbling on rocks and fallen branches. The song of the cicadas was relentless, and there was an image fixed in her mind that kept morphing. At any moment a prowling jaguar or an anaconda that lurked in the undergrowth could be just ahead. But she couldn't think this way. Accessing her programming again, she made herself block out the potential attackers. She had to run, to keep running . . .

Even though I have no idea where I'm going.

Her feet splashed suddenly in water, cool rather than cold but shocking all the same. Unsteadily, Salome came to a halt, breathing hard. Didn't snakes live in water here?

She forged forward, her heart pounding. Was it a lake? A river? There was no way to make out the far bank, but water was surely a good thing to walk in right now. It would help conceal her trail. Salome could feel a faint current against her skin; she turned into it and waded unsteadily against it, upstream. The water was up to her thighs now and growing deeper with every step.

In the distance, despite the night sounds of the jungle creatures, she heard the cracking of branches and the sound of human voices. Panic rose in her chest. *They're coming. Already.*

Splashing farther out into the sluggardly stream, Salome tried to breathe deeply, air moving in and out of her lungs. *If I need to hide under the surface, I'll need plenty of oxygen in my blood. Thanks, IIDA.*

I'm sorry I panicked before, Mother. I won't this time.

Access GPS download. Please, IIDA.

Though it was terrifying to hear her pursuers draw closer, Salome made herself stay perfectly still. She closed her eyes, letting the information stream into her mind in a torrent,

<132>

searching the database in her brain as it loaded. The global map focused and then narrowed: Brazil, Amazonas, the rain forest, the river, its sluggish tributary. *This very spot.* And the topography beneath the river's surface. *They're coming. They're nearly here—*

She suddenly found what she needed. Narrowing her eyes, Salome waded as silently as she could, deeper and deeper, until the water was up to her armpits. *Piranhas. Anacondas.* Salome shuddered and dismissed the thoughts. The pursuing footsteps seemed so close now, more cracking branches. There were shouts and high-pitched yells.

This was it. Taking her deepest breath yet, she submerged herself entirely in the river, twisted, and swam downward.

She could see nothing, but she knew it was there: unerringly, she reached out and found the rocks with her fingertips. *I know it's there. IIDA's GPS won't let me down.*

There. She could sense the gaping hole in the rock, and she continued swimming, though her lungs were bursting now. Clumsily, Salome breaststroked into the underwater cave, her fingers scraping against the submerged rocks. Now the need for oxygen was irresistible. She swam upward until the pressure lessened, twisted onto her back, and then let herself float the last few inches to the surface.

Air! Salome sucked it in like a desperate newborn. There were only a few inches between her and the cavern roof, but it was enough. She puffed air in and out through her mouth, not caring that it tasted of dank waterweed.

Feeling somewhat safe for the first time since she had fled from Lil Joao, Salome let her muscles go limp with relief. Her breathing slowed and steadied. She blinked her eyes open.

<133>

Expecting total darkness, she was surprised by the flicker of blue light, bright as a neon sign. Instantly, she knew what it was, but Salome barely had time to be scared. No doubt, neither did the eel, but there wasn't much space in this underwater cavern. It would hardly be able to keep from stinging her.

Pain racked her body, and Salome screamed out loud, taking in a mouthful of water. Coughing, spluttering, she tried to keep herself calm, but it was impossible. *IIDA, help me!*

Elec   tric eels ca   n't kill   human. No. No—
500–600 volts— safe— painf ul—Ke eep ca—

Inside her head there was nothing but turmoil. Data streams went into overdrive, flickering, tripping, and flashing. Nothing made sense. It was like an electrical storm in her brain, and not just her brain. Salome's limbs jerked like an electrified insect. She felt her feet, hands, and head crash painfully against rock, but there was nothing she could do. Water gushed into her mouth and nose; she spluttered and coughed, only to take in more. Only one thought was clear through the chaos:

Electricity's overloaded the programming. GET OUT.

That wasn't IIDA; IIDA was useless right now. It was her human brain, urging her to live. Frantically, jerkily, Salome gasped in as much air as she could catch, then submerged and swam as hard and fast as she could.

Her strokes, though, were not strong or quick at all. She wanted to swim hard, but it was beyond her. She feebly dragged herself against the rock and out into the open river, her heels dragging against the ragged rock at the cavern entrance. With her lungs almost ready to explode, she kicked one last time,

<134>

as hard as she could. She aimed her weak body toward the air bubbles that leaked upward from her nose and mouth.

Air. Salome gasped in huge lungfuls of it, then flailed her arms and legs. Unable to stand, she thrashed wildly toward the bank. When she finally reached it, she grasped handfuls of weeds and dragged herself out, achingly slowly. Her feet were still dangling in the river, when she went utterly limp, incapable of any more effort. Her body was racked with pain and confusion. If an anaconda or a jaguar found her now, they were welcome to her—

"*Ela está aqui!*"

The shout came from right above her. Despair overwhelmed her; she could do nothing. They might as well shoot her right here.

"*Eu a encontrei!*"

There was no escape, but the least she could do was understand their plans for her. . . . Lost in a sickening sense of defeat, Salome clicked on the translation facility in her mind.

Nothing. She knew at once what had happened. The electric shock had done more than confuse her internal AI; it had shorted it out completely.

There was nothing she could do but give a muffled scream as a black-gloved hand clapped over her mouth. She did not even have enough consciousness to panic.

She was nothing more than Salome Abraham. She was entirely human, entirely helpless.

And they had come for her.

<135>

Twenty-Two

It was hot and damp where John lay, but he sensed even before he opened his eyes that he was no longer in the tree house, or even outside in the jungle. When he did manage to blink his eyelids apart, he could see only darkness. There was an echoing emptiness to the place. *I'm shut in somewhere,* he thought fuzzily.

Reaching out, he felt a limp arm beside him. He moved his hand, and it touched sleek hair. *Eva.* She was breathing but unmoving—unconscious, he realized.

John sat up, his head pounding. Gradually, his eyes were adjusting; he could make out the sheen of faint light on pipes and a metal door. When he reached behind him to touch the wall, it was cool, damp, and earthen. *A cellar of some sort.*

There was something else; he could sense other bodies around him. There was the stir of breathing from several other human beings. John tensed.

At that moment, metal creaked, a crack of light appeared, and the dark room was split by the glow from an open hatch above him. John craned his neck up. Children were walking down the

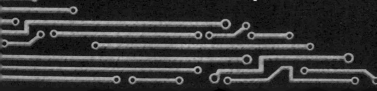

steep, rusty metal steps that led down from the hatch, carrying trays. But that wasn't whom he had felt in the cellar with him.

He could see the other inhabitants clearly now, and they were adults. The men were scruffily bearded, the women lank haired. Their clothes looked stylish but grubby and torn, and everyone's eyes were hollow and afraid. And no wonder—on their heads were fastened odd steel contraptions held tight by clamps. John doubted they were wearing them voluntarily.

"Good morning," said a bright voice.

Mirandinha stalked down the steps, gazing at her captives like a monarch surveying her dutiful peasants. She bestowed a brilliant smile on them all, her eyes coming to rest on John—and on Eva, who was groggily regaining consciousness.

"Mirandinha." John rubbed his temples. "What's happening?"

Beside him Eva was sitting up unsteadily, blinking hard and shaking herself. But it was John who felt he was really, truly waking up. The last week or so seemed like a blurry dream. Mirandinha was an ally, wasn't she? She'd been so helpful and kind—so tolerant of him and his friends' mistakes. She'd welcomed them in, made them feel at home here—

No. No, that's not how it went . . .

"John! Eva! I'm so glad you're awake." Mirandinha watched indulgently as the children set the trays on the earthy floor: bowls of mashed banana that seemed to be mixed with a few grains. It didn't look very appetizing; what had happened to the bountiful selections of tropical fruit, pastries, and French toast? wondered John. He didn't get a chance to ask the children, who trooped back up the steps past Mirandinha without a word.

<137>

Two of the kids, though, stayed on either side of Mirandinha, pistols clutched in their small hands.

"Why are we here?" John asked again. "What's this about?"

Eva, silent, glared murderously at Mirandinha.

"This is the Ma'yaarr Complex, John, as you know," laughed Mirandinha. "And these are your new classmates. Let me introduce you all by name. John Laine and Eva Vygotsky: I want you to meet Errol Braithwaite, Advanced Coding; Beatrisa Dominguez, Data Analysis; Lotte De Vries, Computer Architecture; Marius Anghelescu, Algorithms and Data Structures . . ."

John stared at the silent adults as Mirandinha reeled off their names and subjects. They did not react beyond an occasional sullen nod as their names were mentioned. When Mirandinha had finished, John turned to her in shock.

"These are the teachers from the Complex?"

"Indeed, they are." Mirandinha shrugged. "For what they're worth. The best decision we ever made here was when we realized that this older generation knows less about the new world than we do. Your father, Mikael, is of the same generation, John: stuck in the old ways, lacking imagination. He was useful to you, as these teachers were, briefly, to us, but we have moved on, and so must you. That way of training is outdated. Here at the Ma'yaarr Complex we have taken our education into our own hands, and we have begun to develop AI far faster and further than these dinosaurs would ever have allowed. Why, our methods have already worked on you, to an extent."

John stared at her. *IIDA did try to warn me. And I told her not to be paranoid.*

<138>

Eva staggered to her feet and glowered at the girl. "Now it makes sense. You manipulated John's emotions somehow."

"Not so much his emotions—those are still too human—but his decision-making faculties." Mirandinha smiled. "And it was really quite easy. He kind of *wanted* to be manipulated; didn't you, John? You loved all the attention you got."

John reddened as a wave of shame and fury washed over him.

"Anyway, your AI is your own, John. No more hacking for now. That was only a temporary experiment, and we're done with it."

"Because you've got us where you want us?" seethed Eva.

"Exactly. Now we can proceed with the real project, which is to take the AI prototypes as far as they can go. I believe the potential is limitless. Why should I not apply and progress the AI in brains that are *already* fully developed? All your father wanted, John, was to save children. It was done for his own glory, and it was done so *lazily*—Mikael did the minimum he could get away with. What a waste!"

"And you, Mirandinha?" growled John. "What do you want?"

She spread her arms expansively. "I want to create superheroes, John! That's what we can achieve here—superpowers more relevant and effective than anything in a comic book! You know what your father did, John? He turned you and your friends into mutants. I want to make that worthwhile, and I don't want to restrict the possibilities to adolescents."

"Wait," said Eva suddenly. "You said you wanted to apply the AI to brains that are already . . . *developed.* What are you planning? What do you mean, 'developed'?"

<139>

"I want to change the DNA of perfectly healthy adults," said Mirandinha. "Imagine what I can achieve! If it can be done without consequences—"

"And if it can't?" interrupted John, with a glance at the imprisoned teachers.

Mirandinha shrugged, and a slow grin spread over her face. "So much the better. No harm done to those who matter, right? To those who are the actual *future*."

"These men and women taught you!" exploded Eva. "Are you not even *grateful* that they sparked all these ideas in you? All this ambition?"

"Of course I'm grateful, and I'll be even more grateful when they help me advance my research." Mirandinha turned to the two small children who had stayed behind, and she jerked her head toward the metal door in the wall. "But not all those here are educators. Some are simply special guests . . . who have never had much of a purpose in life."

Eva took a sharp, high breath. John seized her arm and squeezed it in an effort to reassure her.

The two armed and dead-eyed children marched to the metal door. One by one, Lil Joao yanked back bolts, with explosive crashes so loud they made John want to cover his ears.

The last bar came loose with a grinding screech. Lil Joao turned slightly, to give Eva a sly and unpleasant grin. Then he awkwardly cocked his gun, aimed it at the door, and tugged it open.

It swung wide with a menacing creak and clanged against the wall. Lil Joao gave a harsh yell of summons.

<140>

At first there was nothing to see but darkness. Then, with moans of fear, two shadows detached themselves from the lightless gap and crept forward into the dusty dimness of the main cellar.

A man and a woman stood before them, blinking, unsteady, and terrified.

Eva stumbled forward, her eyes wide. John put his hand over his mouth. Here they were, just as Eva's mysterious letter had described them: tall, brown-haired, attractive though dirty from their cramped cellar room. The woman stared ahead and burst into tears. The man, too, put his arm around his wife and began to weep.

But they weren't looking at Eva. Their red eyes were riveted on Mirandinha.

"Those people." Eva was breathing hard. "They are not my parents?"

"Hah!" exclaimed Mirandinha. "No, but they were a good way to get you down to Brazil, weren't they? I guess these two had to be useful for *something*. Oh, don't get upset, Eva. I can assure you they are completely useless at being parents. You wouldn't want them."

The woman gave a gasp of distress; the man took a step toward his daughter, but one of the small children, growling, jabbed him back into place with the pistol barrel.

"Lil Joao found them wandering in the rain forest," said Mirandinha, with a contemptuous glance at her parents. "They'd never have found their way in otherwise, though I gave them every clue you could imagine." She rolled her eyes. "After that, it was easy enough to get a fabricated story to Sarah Lopez.

<141>

She's always thirsty for a good exclusive, isn't she? To the point she'll believe anything. Though, actually, I suppose that's true of you too." She grinned at Eva.

Eva gave a strangled snarl of grief and lunged at Mirandinha; John grabbed her and dragged her back before Lil Joao could raise his pistol.

"And thank you for bringing John Laine, in particular," she told Eva. "I especially want to clone those abilities of his. You, Eva, you're a bit of a loose cannon, though we will still be using you—but John is sleekly efficient, isn't he?" Mirandinha's cold eyes traveled over John from head to foot. "Pity the other girl got away, but she won't get far. If she lives, we'll use her too. We'll test all your skills and capacities on new subjects, see what effect they have on a fully formed brain stem." She gave the teachers a sly glance. "The experiments will begin tomorrow—better sooner than later, I always say!"

Eva clenched and unclenched her fists. "I am willing to bet these experiments of yours are dangerous. Am I right? Dangerous and no doubt painful."

Mirandinha smirked. "Maybe."

"And Ana?" snapped Eva. "What's happened to her, or is she in some other cellar? Or was she just one of your minions, luring us down here from the Wolf's Den?"

Mirandinha roared with laughter. "Ana? Oh, she was lovely wasn't she? I *liked* being Ana; it was like inhabiting another soul!"

Eva gave a cry of pain, clutching her head. At exactly the same moment, John felt the sharp and hot sting of his MindReader, as if someone had electrified the messaging system.

<142>

—Remember me? 🌺 💝 🐢 🌳 😊 😊 😊 😊 Sweet eco-friendly Ana! 😺 👾

"Well, it's time to say good night," Mirandinha told them mockingly, as Eva and John rubbed their heads and grimaced. "We'll get through the A-B testing phases by midday, I should imagine."

She marched back up the stairs, the metal clanging, and Lil Joao and his fierce-eyed friend followed her, menacingly eyeing the cellar's inhabitants. The hatch slammed shut behind them, and the cellar was in almost total darkness once again.

John could barely make out the adults falling on the grim-looking food, and he could certainly hear them, but he and Eva did not eat.

"I can't believe I fell for her," said Eva in a low voice.

"Easily done." John slumped down onto the floor. "I fell for her harder than you or Salome did."

Eva sat down beside him. "But Salome got away! There's some hope."

"Until they find her." John sighed. "I guess I was too cocky with the MindReader—I thought we'd developed a real thing that could read minds. But it's nothing more than the internet in your head.

"And just like the internet, anyone can pretend to be something they aren't."

<143>

Twenty-Three

"Good morning," Eva muttered to John.

He sat up, groggily, still seeing nothing but darkness. "How can you tell?"

"I can hear the birds outside. And the frogs have shut up." As John's eyes adjusted again, he saw her shrug. "John, how on earth did Mirandinha know about me? She knew exactly where to find me and how to convince me to come running down here. Did I meet her somewhere, confide in her? But I just don't remember!"

"And I wonder what the deal is with her parents," muttered John. He glanced over to where they sat with the other adults.

Eva got to her feet. "I am going to ask them. They owe us an explanation, since they are partly responsible for Mirandinha." She sounded grim.

John got to his feet and followed her as she marched across the cellar. Eva stopped in front of the couple and stood glaring, her arms folded.

"What made you come here?"

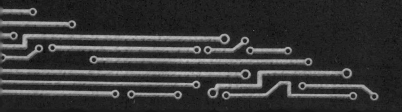

They glanced up, looking shocked. Then they exchanged a look of misery. The man muttered to his wife, and she raised her head to Eva.

"*É um longo . . . e triste conto*," began the woman, haltingly.

Eva shook her head impatiently. "I don't speak Portuguese. You speak Russian? French or English?"

The man touched his wife's arm. "I speak English. My wife, Juliana . . . as she says, it is a long and sad story. My name is Francisco Pereira dos Santos. We came here to search for our daughter . . ."

"So that part was true, at least," muttered Eva.

Juliana spoke rapidly to her husband, and he nodded.

"We lost contact with Mirandinha, not long after she came to the Ma'yaarr Complex," explained Francisco. "She would not reply to messages—and when she did, she replied very strangely; we barely understood what she was saying. We thought . . . that she was being how do you say it—played? Controlled?"

"Manipulated," said John, bitterly.

"Just so. Manipulated." Francisco nodded. "Eventually, Mirandinha stopped calling us. No more contact at all, and the school seemed unwilling to help. None of the teachers would reply to us, none of the staff. Nothing but silence."

Juliana nodded, watching her husband eagerly. "*E depois . . .*" She was not always comfortable speaking English.

"Yes. Then we received a call—from a stranger, how do you say . . . out of the blue. They said something had gone wrong at the Ma'yaarr Complex. That Mirandinha was still there. But it was all this person would tell us. They would say nothing more. If we came here and someone asked, we were to tell them Roy Lykos sent us."

<145>

"Lykos!" A cold chill raced through John's body along with a nauseating sense of inevitability. Eva clutched his hand and squeezed it, but he wasn't comforting. *I should have known. All along. How could I have imagined prison would stop him?*

Francisco looked from Eva to John, guilty and a little ashamed. "This name—Lykos—it was respected at the time; we had no doubts. I myself admired him very much. I was impressed to know he was involved here. Juliana and I set out right away."

John nodded. "Don't feel bad. He fooled a lot of people."

"We wanted to save our daughter," said Francisco dully. "We thought we were coming to help her. We had no idea the Complex was in trouble because *our daughter* had taken over. We did not . . . we did not even know she was capable of such a thing."

"You didn't know her very well, then," said Eva.

Juliana seemed to understand that, at least. She gave a small cry of despair. "*Não.*"

"We were too busy," lamented Francisco. "We thought we were doing what was best for Mirandinha, when, in fact, we were too busy to know her properly. I can understand why she has lashed out in resentment." He murmured something to Juliana, who nodded in agreement.

"I don't think it's your fault. Not entirely," blurted John. He shot a look at the disapproving Eva. "I get mad at my father too. He's always busy, never has time for me. Yet he's given me everything. Sounds like you gave Mirandinha an awful lot."

"Perhaps too much," muttered Francisco. "Everything but our attention."

John felt a stab of remorse. They were wrong about Mirandinha, Mikael was wrong about John—but he, too, was wrong about his father. *About a lot of things.* He'd been quite sure he

<146>

hated Mikael. He certainly resented his father for all he'd done to him. Yet now John found himself wishing desperately that he was here. Mikael would know exactly what to do. *And he did his best. He's always done his best for me, even when I didn't want it . . .*

I thought I was like Mirandinha, but I'm not. I couldn't do what she's done to her parents. At least I know that now.

I don't want to end up like Mirandinha—with no family even to argue with. We've got to try harder for each other, Dad. . . . You and me both.

His MindReader had been taken; there was no way to contact his father. Maybe it was too late to tell him how he really felt. Mirandinha's plans hadn't sounded as if they would end well for John or for her parents . . .

The hatch to the cellar was suddenly flung open, flooding the dark space with hot light. Mirandinha stood silhouetted against it, her arms triumphantly folded.

"I have you all where I want you," she announced with satisfaction. "Now we can begin."

<<>>

Salome's head hurt, with a ringing pain that was like nothing she had ever felt before. The best way she could describe it was white noise: white noise that stung and burned. There was no thinking that could be done. Her mind was a mass of confused code and meaningless prompts. Somewhere far beyond her chaotic brain, low voices talked urgently, but she could not understand them. They made no sense.

All she had left was instinct, and that was almost subsumed in racing lines of churning code. Lashing out with the last of her inner strength, she did all that she was capable of:

```
/syscall/Akane/syscall/Slack man/locate/
/man/HELP
```

Twenty-Four

The lab was far too bright after their day and night in the dimness of the cellar. John blinked hard as he was led in, his eyes stinging, but he could make out the most important details. It was cold and clinical, all safety glass and stainless steel, and there were banks of monitors and hard drives arranged against one wall. The polished floor was clear except for two sleek chairs, like dentists' chairs, that faced each other across an empty space. The chairs were linked by cables.

A nervous-looking adult technician turned to John. "This is him?"

Mirandinha nodded triumphantly. "This is indeed *him*. We can begin." With a hand on John's shoulder, she shoved him down into the chair. One of the child guards clicked the wrist and ankle restraints closed.

Lil Joao shoved Juliana into the opposite chair, then fastened her restraints. John stared at Mirandinha's mother, a slowly rising dread churning in his chest. Juliana looked terrified.

"What's going on?" she demanded uncomfortably.

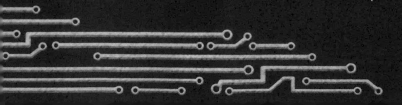

"Nothing you need to concern yourself about," snapped Mirandinha. "You are not the scientist here; you are the test subject." She smirked at her mother.

The technician stabbed at a keyboard, glancing anxiously at Mirandinha. "What level?"

Mirandinha spun to face John. Her eyes searched his face. "Maximum," she snarled.

"Oh no, Mirandinha." The technician hugged a clipboard, his eyes widening. "That's not possible, I'm afraid. Mr. Lykos explained that anything beyond level 13 could kill both of them."

"Whom did Mr. Lykos put in charge of this project?" snapped Mirandinha at the technician. "Me or you?"

"You, Mirandinha—I'm sorry, but—"

"Then do as you're told! We have two carrier subjects, do we not? And many, many more receptacles." Her eyes flashed. "We are pressed for time now. Get it done: maximum level. *Now.*"

John stopped straining against the metal restraints; what was the point? He shut his eyes tight. *I wish I had never come here. I wish I'd told Dad where we were going. I wish I'd told him I loved him before I got killed in a dentist chair, shoot. I wonder where Eva is and what they're doing to her? They marched her off, god knows where . . .*

At least Salome got away . . .

John's eyes burned, and his stomach churned, more with rage than fear. There was a soft whine close to him; he blinked open his eyes to see a long needle whirring toward his forehead. It was so close it was swiftly out of focus. All he could see was a dazzling haze of white light, fury, and terror; all he could hear was that earsplitting whine of the needle. Its point pricked his forehead.

<149>

There was another sound, and he didn't even want to know what it was. It was like an explosion, a loud crack, and it was followed by yells and a pounding that might be the blood throbbing in his head.

A black gloved hand seized the needle, tearing it aside, and he felt the restraints go loose.

What the—

He felt himself lifted from the chair and slung over a strong shoulder. Glancing fuzzily around, he saw Juliana, too, being dragged from her chair by a black-clad figure. *What's Mirandinha doing—?*

A volley of shouting surrounded him as he was quickly carried out of the lab and slung down in the corridor beyond. He staggered, just keeping his footing. He was surrounded by those black-clad figures, but none were taking any notice of him; their guns were leveled at Mirandinha and her child soldiers in the lab. Juliana was shouting something, desperate and scared, as she tried to clutch at one of the guns. "*Não a mate! Não a mate!* Don't kill her!"

"We won't." A gloved hand pushed her back. "*Fique atrás!* Stay back!"

Mirandinha was snarling, shouting orders. The children, looking utterly unafraid, pointed their guns at the invaders, shrieking defiance. Lil Joao darted out of the lab and flung something to the floor.

There was a crack, a flash of light, and for a moment John thought the boy had thrown a grenade. But as the nearest Kevlar-suited attackers fell back, stunned, he realized it was only

<150>

a sonic boom. The attackers were scrambling to their feet, taking cover from Lil Joao's fire.

The black-clad figure who had carried John from the lab growled something unintelligible, gripped his arm, and dragged him away along the corridor. John wanted to resist, but for the moment this made sense: *Get far from the lab. That's all that matters. Then get away from these attackers next.*

He sprinted up the corridor and swung around a corner, hoping to outpace his new captor. But the figure was right on his heels, jerking the gun in an unmistakable gesture of threat, driving him farther from the others.

Worry later! Get away!

He didn't even know whether this was a friend or an enemy—

Process data—process data—analyze.

There wasn't time even for IIDA to analyze anything. As they both staggered to a halt around the next corner, the paramilitary ripped off her protective helmet. And shook her braids loose.

"Salome?" gasped John.

"Come on! Let's get out of here!" Dragging him, she set off once again at a run.

"The others?" he panted, glancing back.

"They're cops. They'll deal with those kids, and they won't have to harm them. *Not that I'd care!*" Salome put on a burst of furious speed, and he raced to keep pace with her. Juliana and the other captives pounded after them with cries of panic.

Already the shots behind them had stopped. Lil Joao and his cohort must have surrendered, thought John, because for all the kid's psychotic aggression, he didn't have the firepower to outgun the police. *But what about Mirandinha—*

<151>

No. Lil Joao was a distraction!

Well, he couldn't see Mirandinha, and he wasn't about to go back to the lab to check on her. Rounding a corner after Salome, he followed her out of the outer door that now hung loose from its hinges. She sprinted toward the river and the dock.

"Get in!" she commanded, raising her gun to cover them as she gestured at one of the moored boats.

John and Eva and the other "subjects" didn't need to be told twice. Mirandinha, John saw as he glanced back, had indeed left Lil Joao and his cohort to their fate; she was striding out of the Complex, her face rigid with fury.

Another black-uniformed cop threw himself into the boat and keyed the engine to life as Salome scrambled in last. The boat veered sharply away from the jetty, its wake foaming behind it.

Clutching the gunwale, John stared at Mirandinha, still striding determinedly along the jetty. He expected her to leap for a boat and come in pursuit, but she only halted, glaring, and snapped the fingers of both hands.

John glanced down at the water, his heart plummeting. Through the churning of the wake, he saw red lights spark to life. Pairs of them shot through the water after the boat at lightning speed.

"The fish!" he yelled to Salome. "The robot fish!"

"Faster!" she yelled to the cop.

John gripped the gunwale for his dear life; he was sure the bow was going to lift out of the water and flip in a deadly somersault. Tiny white streaks headed toward the boat—those little torpedoes that could damage it.

<152>

But as John desperately peered back, he realized the boat was outpacing the robots. The white underwater trails fizzled and died. The twin red lights dwindled behind the boat like markers on a highway and at last blinked out.

Mirandinha gave a scream of frustrated fury that reached them even over the roar of the engine. She reached down and seized something at her feet.

"*Baixa!*" yelled the cop, yanking Salome down as the rest ducked. But the rattle of machine gun bullets pinged and zipped on the water behind them. They were out of range.

Eva jumped to her feet and gave Mirandinha a heartfelt gesture of contempt.

"Take that!"

There was a roar and rattle overhead. John shaded his eyes and stared into the blue sky above the canopy. A whole fleet of helicopters was heading for the Complex; he could make out black and white lettering on their flanks that said *Polícia*.

"And that," said Eva with satisfaction, as she slumped down against the gunwale, "is the end of Mad Mirandinha."

<153>

Twenty-Five

"Mirandinha was wrong about everything," John told Salome as they walked through Manaus Airport. "She kept telling me you were weak, but you're the strongest of us all."

Salome gave him a nod and a grin. "And don't you forget it, boy child!"

"I dread to think what would have happened if you hadn't made that run for it." John hitched his pack higher on his shoulder. He shuddered at the memory of that oncoming needle.

"Try not to think about it," said Salome. "You'll just have nightmares. Hey, there's your dad!"

John felt his heart sink as he stared at the waiting figure beyond the arrivals gate. Mikael was waving furiously. There were two smaller figures at his side, not waving but grinning broadly.

"Akane!" yelled Eva. "Slack!" She jogged ahead, and the two seemed to step apart as they hurried forward for a hug.

"Hey," muttered Salome with a grin, "were Akane and Slack standing really close there?"

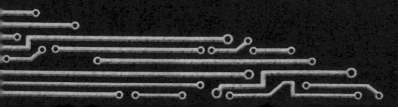

John narrowed his eyes. "I thought they were holding hands, but I could be seeing things . . ."

"John!" As they walked beyond the barrier, Mikael stepped forward and embraced him in a bear hug.

"I'm sorry, Dad," John blurted, muffled by Mikael's shoulder. "Sorry we ran off like that."

"John, don't." Mikael hugged him tight. "It was my fault too."

"Not gonna argue," mumbled John. "You were pretty unbearable."

Mikael gave a dry laugh. "I was too obsessed with the school, and I just assumed you'd be OK with everything. I should have communicated more. I'm just glad you're OK. All three of you."

John detached himself from his father's embrace, enough to hug Akane and Slack in turn. "Did these guys tell you everything?" he asked his father.

"Not so much," laughed Slack. "He found out just as we realized you were in trouble."

Mikael looked shamefaced. "Your mother, John. Tina was livid with me when I told her you'd gone. Said I was self-obsessed and I needed to stop with the stupid 'spy games' and tell her what was going on." His eyes narrowed. "Not that I wasn't mad with you and Slack about that fictitious Shanghai conference."

"Yeah." John stared at his shoes. "Sorry, Dad."

"If it hadn't been for Salome, you'd have been dead meat," said Akane. "Thank God she got a message to us—and it wasn't easy, apparently. But once we alerted Mikael and Mikael alerted Interpol, the Brazilian cops swung into action."

"And found me," pointed out Salome.

<155>

"You attacked the compound at exactly the right moment," said John, rubbing his forehead.

"Yeah. My AI was so screwed up I couldn't even say a nursery rhyme." Salome grinned.

"You didn't need it, did you? You got through to Akane and Slack somehow, and I want to hear about it later. Meanwhile, you're my hero," said John with feeling. He rubbed his forehead again, almost feeling the sting of that needle.

"And they let me join the assault—actually, they encouraged me to. That was kinda fun. I want to be a police officer now."

"You'd make a great one." Mikael clapped Salome's shoulder. "As for John, what can I expect from mixing teenage hormones and advanced AI?" He winked at John. "Have some candy to show all's forgiven."

John reached into the offered package and popped one into his mouth.

"Ahhh, it's disgusting!" He spat it into his hand.

"Durian flavor," grinned Salome, as the others, too, made faces and spat out their candies. "Fortunately, I like it."

"Four out of five ain't bad for revenge," laughed Mikael, nudging Slack. "You're not the only ones who can play practical jokes. And it's sweet justice that I picked them up in Shanghai."

Slack made a wry face. "Fair enough."

"You know, I'll miss the Amazon," sighed Salome, chewing.

"Slack and I never even got to see it," pointed out Akane, mournfully.

"Oh, you didn't miss that much," laughed John. "The only fish Salome got to swim with were hostile robots!"

<156>

"And an electric eel," Salome reminded him with a shiver. "I won't be doing *that* again."

John glanced at Akane and Slack as they walked ahead of them toward the parking garage. He was *sure* their hands were in contact.

"Salome," he muttered with a grin, "I guess you're not the only one who got an electric charge this term."

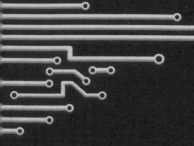

Epilogue

Roy Lykos clasped his hands in front of him on the chipped metal desk. He closed his eyes. Sometimes he was very glad he was so adept at meditation.

Not that he would let his emotions get the better of him.

"I'm sorry things didn't work out this time, Roy," murmured Evan J. Whiteford. He was pacing up and down, his hands behind his back. He needed, thought Roy, to be calmer. Think clinically, just as Roy himself did. Why was he surrounded by overemotional incompetents?

"So near," he told Evan, his eyes still closed, "yet so far. There will be future opportunities."

"They won't be at the Ma'yaarr Complex," growled Evan. "The Brazilian Polícia have, in their infinite wisdom, closed it down until further notice."

"There are other Centers," murmured Roy.

"With students as malleable as young Mirandinha?" Evan spread his hands.

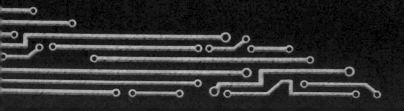

"You know what I like about Mikael's DNA technology?" smiled Roy. "It makes everyone malleable. As dear Mirandinha discovered with John Laine."

"Still." Evan frowned. "Mikael has cooperated with Interpol and opened up his network to them."

"I think we can almost discount Mikael as a player. There's another person who should have interested me more from the start. A version 1.0. If only I'd thought to keep her closer and study her in more detail, I could have retro-engineered every step Mikael took along the way."

"You'll find it hard to get your hands on Eva now," pointed out Evan.

"Oh, I don't think so. Easiest thing in the world." Roy leaned back, his hands behind his head. "You see, it's clear now what she wants most in the world.

"And since I know exactly what happened on that Trans-Siberian Express, and how, and why . . . well, Evan." Roy Lykos smiled in triumph. "I'm the one person in the world who can give Eva Vygotsky exactly what she wants."

. . . update available . . .
. . . downloading . . .

<159>

Look for these books!

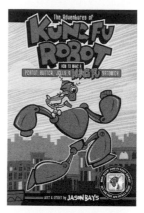

Listen up! Enjoy *The Ghost Network* series in audio, wherever audiobooks are sold.